THE BRIDE PRICE

ALSO BY BUCHI EMECHETA

Novels

Second-Class Citizen
The Slave Girl
The Joys of Motherhood
Double Yoke
The Rape of Shavi
The Family

Young Adult Novels

The Wrestling Match
The Moonlight Bride

THE BRIDE PRICE

a novel by

Buchi Emecheta

George Braziller
New York

Originally published in Britain
by Allison & Busby Limited

First published in the United States of America
by George Braziller, Inc., in 1976

For information, please address the publisher:
George Braziller, Inc.
171 Madison Avenue
New York, NY 10016
www.georgebraziller.com

Library of Congress Cataloging-in-Publication Data:
Emecheta, Buchi.
    The bride price.
    I. Title.
PZ4.E525Br 3   [PR9387.9.E36]   823   75-46608

ISBN-13: 978-0-8076-0951-4
ISBN-10: 0-8076-0951-X

Printed and bound in the United States of America

Fifteenth paperback printing, 2006

Contents

12.71

For my mother
Alice Ogbanje Emecheta

I

The Bride Price

Aku-nna fitted the key into the keyhole, turned it this way and that, pushed open the whitewashed door, then stood there, very still. For right there in the middle of the room was their father, staring back at them, wordlessly. He stood there, hat in hand, properly khakied in his work clothes and looking very much like a guilty criminal caught stealing.

Aku-nna and her brother Nna-nndo stepped inside their one-room apartment, still staring at him, mutely demanding explanation. *You ought to be at work,* their silent gazes seemed to be saying. *You ought not to be here; you ought to be at the Loco yard with your mates, not here standing in the middle of the room scaring us so.* But if their father had any explanations to make, he was biding his time.

The boy Nna-nndo was eleven. He was tall for his age, with the narrow build of his mother. At school he had just started to use ink and this he was determined to let everybody know. Writing with ink was to him an academic achievement, for though he was very clever at other arts he was very slow in book work. His fingers were always smeared with ink; it oozed from its bottle onto his hands, some onto his khaki school uniform. Some he even rubbed on his close woolly curls, and if you asked him why he did that, he would reply: "Ink makes my hair blacker." He had a good sense of humour, just like their mother, Ma Blackie.

Ma Blackie was a giant of a woman. She was so tall and straight that her few enemies called her "the palm-tree woman". Her jet black skin had earned her the nickname "Blackie the Black" when she was a little girl, and nothing about her had changed much now that she had a family of her own. In fact her blackness was even glossier. So her neighbours and friends added the respectful title "Ma" to her name, and she became "Ma Blackie" not only to her children but to all. If you came down to Akinwunmi Street and said you were looking for a "Ma", which title many women shared, your informer would probably ask, "Could it be that you mean Ma Blackie?"

But Ma Blackie, though always laughing and loudly cheerful, had a family problem. She was very slow in getting herself pregnant again. Since her husband returned from Burma, when the war ended some five years before, she had not been pregnant like other wives whose husbands had gone abroad to fight Hitler. Her husband, Ezekiel Odia, had sent her to all the native doctors he could afford in Lagos, but still no more children. He even encouraged her to join the Cherubim and Seraphim sect. These people babbled their prayers to God in a frenzied kind of way, but to no avail. Ma Blackie was not pregnant. In despair she decided to go home to their town, Ibuza, to placate their Oboshi river goddess into giving her some babies.

While Ma Blackie was in Ibuza recharging her fertility, Aka-nna and Nna-nndo were left to take care of themselves and their father. Ezekiel Odia, whom they often called "Nna", the Ibo word for father, was to keep his job at the Loco yard where he worked as a head moulder. This position of responsibility had been given to him out of respect for the fact that he had been to the war, and he guarded it with his very soul. He would wake very early each morning, bustling himself about their one room, waking everyone else up, in his haste dropping this, picking up that, shouting for the other in his little voice. In size he was a little man, too, and people wondered how he had come to marry such a giant of a woman. The answer maybe was that like most Ibo men of his generation he had taken his wife when she was still a young girl; the trouble with Ezekiel's bride was that she seemed never to stop growing. However, such natural imbalance did nothing to disrupt the marriage. All it did was to make Ezekiel Odia acquire a funny way of standing on his toes when making a point.

So on this particular day when his two children had sped home from school, expecting to be greeted by an empty room as usual, they were stunned to see him, standing there flat on his feet, in the centre of the room, his eyes bloodshot, with tiny red worm-like criss-crosses in them. He was nervously twisting and retwisting his old felt hat, uncertain still of what he was going to tell his children and of how to begin.

Aku-nna came closer to him. She was only thirteen, but she had realised quite a while before that all was not well in her family. Many a time she had heard other women living in the same compound make songs of her Ma Blackie's childlessness. She had heard over and over again her Ma Blackie and her Nna quarrelling over this great issue of childlessness. Nna would go on and on, talking in that small, sad voice of his, telling Ma, reminding her, that he had had to pay double the normal bride price before he was able to take Ma as his wife. He would work himself up, his little voice whining like a hungry dog's, and then drawing himself up on tiptoe, maybe hoping to add to his stature by so doing, he would remind Ma Blackie that having paid this heavy bride price he had had their marriage sanctified by Anglicanism. And what had he to show for it all — an only son!

Aku-nna knew that she was too insignificant to be regarded as a blessing to this unfortunate marriage. Not only was she a girl but she was much too thin for the approval of her parents, who would rather have a strong and plump little girl for a daughter. Aku-nna just would not put on weight, and this made her look as if she was being starved; but she simply had not the kind of healthy appetite her brother Nna-nndo had. And that was not the end of the disgrace she was showering on her family. If a child at the other end of Akinwunmi Street had chicken-pox, Aku-nna was bound to catch it; if someone else at the bottom of the yard had malaria, Aku-nna would have her share too. For her it was forever a story of today foot, tomorrow head, the day after neck, so much so that her mother many a time begged her to decide once and for all whether she was going to live or die. One thing Ma Blackie could not stand, she said over and over again, was a "living dead", an *ogbanje*.

Ezekiel Odia often pitied his daughter, particularly because she took more after him than his Amazon of a wife. She was small, Aku-nna was, not so much in height as in bone structure, and she was not at all dark, her skin that kind of pale brown colour one gets after putting too much milk in chocolate. Her eyes were large like her father's, but open and translucent; their brownness always had a special glow when she was happy and excited and when she was sad the glimmer disappeared. She had not developed the red criss-crosses which her father had in the whites of his eyes, but Ezekiel knew that, except for the fact that she promised to be a

9

fairly tall woman, his daughter was his very image. He had named her Aku-nna, meaning literally "father's wealth", knowing that the only consolation he could count on from her would be her bride price. To him this was something to look forward to.

Aku-nna on her part was determined not to let her father down. She was going to marry well, a rich man of whom her father would approve and who would be able to afford an expensive bride price. She would have her marriage first of all solemnised by the beautiful goddess of Ibuza, then the Christians would sing her a wedding march — "Here comes the bride" — then her father Nna would call up the spirits of his great, great-grandparents to guide her, then after all that, and only after all that, she would leave her father's house.

But on this hot day, when the sun was pouring its merciless fire onto the unprotected heads of children coming home from school, when the heat was so intense that the ground looked as though it had been cooked and then baked, when the heat ate its way through the shoeless feet of Africans padding their various ways to their various destinations, when the air was so still, so waterless, so juiceless, that perspiration had to pour from the bodies of humans to neutralise the temperature — Aku-nna forgot all thoughts of her bride price, and felt a kind of closeness to which she could not give name binding her to her father. She moved nearer to him, and watched a big bead of perspiration working its way, snake-like, down the bridge of Nna's nose; reaching the wide part where his nose formed two black, funnel-like nostrils, this big stream of perspiration hesitated for a while, then, just like the great River Niger breaking into tributaries, divided into tinier strands. One or two of the tiny strands dropped onto Nna's mouth. He did not lick them, but wiped them away.

Then he spoke, his voice very thick: "They want me to come to the hospital to see to my foot. I shall not be long. I shall be back for the evening meal."

The children looked down at their father's ailing foot. That stupid foot, Aku-nna thought to herself, always gave her father a great deal of trouble. It was the effect of the war. That much she had been told by many of their relatives, especially old Uncle Richard who had been to the war as well. But he was more communicative than their father. Uncle Richard told the children that the white British could not bear the swamp in Burma and India and so they made West African soldiers stand in for them. Their father was lucky to come back alive, he told the children, because many African soldiers died, not from Hitler's bombs but from the conditions they were subjected to. They were either eaten up by the mosquitoes in the Burmese jungle or bitten up by water snakes in India. Aku-nna did not know which of these calamities had actually beefallen her father, but one of his feet had a nasty scar that had healed badly and this foot had a way of getting swollen at any change in weather. It had been plastered over, it had been injected with many medicines by the railway doctor, it had been prayed upon, but it still swelled up at odd times. Now the leg had started to cause Nna pain again and this strain showed however much he tried to hide it. There was a slight swelling in the other foot, too, but both feet were shod in a pair of khaki work shoes and did not look at all bad compared to the way they usually were during the rainy season. So why did Nna seem so unhappy? If all he was going to do was to go to the hospital on Lagos Island for a check up, and if he would be back for the evening meal, then why was he looking so guilty, so disturbed?

Aku-nna did not ask her father this aloud, but the thought was there in her mind, muddled but persistent. She sighed with relief, though, that there was no cause for alarm. Nna would be back for the evening meal. If she had been a grown-up she would have scolded him, saying, "But you scared us so! Standing there as if you have seen a ghost." However in Nigeria you are not allowed to speak in that way to an adult, especially your father. That is against the dictates of culture. Despite that, some little maternal instinct in her told her that he could do with a bit of reassurance. She was now so close that she could touch him.

She laid her small hand on one of his and said, "I'm going to make you Nsala soup, very hot, with lots of pepper, and the pounded yam I shall prepare to go with it will be lumpless. So, Nna, hurry back home to eat your evening meal hot. I know you don't like it cold."

Nna smiled. His reddened eyes focused on his daughter, the corners of the eyes formed small wrinkles and his white teeth gleamed. For a while the woebegone expression on his sick and bloated face disappeared.

"Thank you, my little daughter, but don't boil more yams than you can pound. That *odo* handle is too heavy for you. Don't do too

11

much pounding." He picked up his felt work hat, which he had put on a chair, and adjusted it on his shaved head, pulling the brim down a little in front of his eyes and then padding the sides into shape. "The key to the big cupboard is in my grey trousers — you know, the ones hanging on the hook on the wall. If you want any money, you take it from the big cupboard, but be very careful how you spend it, because you have to make it go a very long way."

If the children thought to themselves, "But you'll be coming back in time for the evening meal tonight," they were now too frightened to say. For not only would it be rude, but also Nna's face, after his brief smile, had assumed the finality of a closed door. He became brisk, just like someone preparing for a final departure. His hands, blackened by years of working in the railway foundry, touched this and that, picking things up and putting them down again. He told them to be good children to their mother and to respect all adults. He told them that they should try to be a glory to his name, because he cared for them, because they were his life.

Eventually Nna came to the door, saying that he had to go now. Then he added: "Always remember that you are mine."

His small lips were shaking and he pressed them together as if he was trying desperately to hold himself from crying. Involuntarily, as if hypnotised against their will, the children drew nearer, their young eyes following the movements of their father's eyes, which by now had grown so big that they seemed to be standing out in relief on his black forehead rather than inside his head. He acted as if in a hurry. He patted Nna-nndo on his inky head, touched Aku-nna slightly on the cheek and went out of the door.

The children followed him, wanting to beg him to wait, to explain what it all meant, this secrecy, these valedictory sighs, this sadness. But Nna did not wait. He hurried as though the gods were calling him, as though the call was imminent and he must answer or be damned.

The children stood there on the veranda, holding the pillars for support, cooling their hot cheeks on the cemented surfaces, and simply stared.

Nna crossed the untarred road in front of their house, his brown canvas shoes making grating sounds on the red hot pebbles. A mammy-wagon lumbered its way from the other end of the street,

12

groaning under the weight of the timber tied on its back. The timbermen, who held onto the big ropes with which the timber was tied, groaned with the wagon, perspiring profusely on their shiny, naked backs. As the wagon rumbled past it blew up a cloud of dust in its wake, covering Nna up. He did not turn to see if his children were watching him, he just went on. The dust from the lorry obscured him completely, and when at last it cleared it seemed to have eaten him up, just as that prophet Elijah in the Bible was eaten up in his chariot of fire.

The road soon cleared. Its red colour snaked between the one-storey houses and came to an abrupt end in front of the big house known locally as The Club.

The children watched the emptiness of the road for a while, felt some pangs of hunger and decided that it was time they went in to eat.

"Always remember that you are mine," Nna had told them.

2

Death

Nna had not yet come back as he had promised he would do. Aku-nna had prepared the evening meal and waited patiently, hoping her father would praise her efforts at cooking when he returned. She had really put more energy than usual into pounding that yam, making quite sure it was nice and smooth before removing it from the heavy wooden mortar. Then she had waited quietly, by the bowl of pounded yam and the freshly made Nsala soup, for Nna. Nna did not come home.

It would soon be getting very dark, and Aku-nna and her brother had never slept all alone in their room before. She was beginning to get worried, and decided that if Nna stayed any longer she was going to tell their neighbours. Their neighbours would look after them, she knew, for in that part of the world everyone is responsible for the next person.

She was sitting cross-legged between the two pillars on the veranda, watching people pass on their way to fetch water for the morning, when she saw a figure who looked like Uncle Uche walking slowly towards the house. Uncle Uche, the son of Nna's elder brother, was also a small man, but unlike Nna he never hurried. In fact Uche's leisurely attitude to life had been the cause of a big quarrel between him and Nna — so big that they had come to blows and Uche had had to leave their house to go and live with friends. Aku-nna had not seen him since, and that had been a long time ago. Now here he was coming towards their house; and, to cap it all, Uncle Joseph was walking with him.

Aku-nna did not know how to welcome them. Nna did not like Uncle Uche, and as for Uncle Joseph — he was known as the local newspaper. He did nothing but talk about other people's business all the time. Ma Blackie once said that if Joseph came to visit you and you gave him a calabash of palm wine, he would go

14

away and tell everybody that you were so poor you didn't even have a glass and could not afford to offer him beer. Ma Blackie also said that if a woman was well dressed Joseph would go and tell his friends he was sure the woman had another man beside her husband. So Aku-nna was afraid of Uncle Joseph's tongue; only God knew what story he was likely to make up about anyone. She was relieved that the two of them, Uche and Joseph, had chosen to pay a visit while Nna was not in, for you could never tell with Nna's temper. He might have thrown a knife at them or something like that.

She scrambled up and ran to meet them. So happy was she at least to see relatives to whom she could confide her present worries that she forgot all about the tale-bearing weakness of Uncle Joseph and the laziness of Uncle Uche. She told them without being asked that her brother Nna-nndo was still out playing, that he was only out so late because he knew Nna had gone to the hospital on the island for a check-up.

"You'd think Nna is going to be there the whole day, the way Nna-nndo is behaving," she said. "He'll be told off, when Nna comes back."

She paused and looked at her uncles, but could read nothing from their faces. They seemed a little solemn perhaps, though she did not mind. Sometimes adults just were sad, and when you asked them why they would say that you were too young to understand or that good children don't ask too many questions. If she was too young to know the meaning of their subdued expressions Aku-nna was not too young to babble on of her hopes that her father would be back soon. For had she not cooked the evening meal specially? Leading the men into the room, she showed them the pounded yam and hot Nsala soup she had prepared, explaining that she had covered the food carefully with Ma Blackie's best antimacassar because her father did not like his meal cold.

Uncle Uche did not smile; he sat down wearily, telling her that she had done very well. Uncle Joseph, for his part, looked at her with something like concern as he lowered himself onto one of their brown chairs, chairs that were high-backed and primitive in structure. He said he wanted water, so Aku-nna scuttled to the shelf behind the curtain and brought out Ma's best tumbler, which was made from a cut bottle since proper drinking glasses were still in short supply after the war. She poured some water

15

from their earthenware water cooler, which had palm-tree patterns all over it, and gave the tumbler to Uncle Joseph. He drank in quick gulps, his Adam's apple flicking up and down as he swallowed, and then asked for more. He must be very thirsty, Aku-nna thought to herself as she hurried to comply, praying that Uncle Uche would not want some too, otherwise there would be no cool water left for Nna when he came home. Thank goodness, Uncle Uche did not think of asking for water; but what he did say was very unwelcome to her.

"Your Nna will not be coming back tonight. He is going to stay at the hospital for a while. They are trying to find out what is wrong with his feet to make them swell so — whether it is because of a snake bite, or because the swamp he was made to stand in for so long when he was fighting in Burma has made the bones rotten. He will not stay very long, but it is better that they find out the cause now and treat it, rather than let him be in the type of endless pain he has been going through these past days. I shall be staying with you until your Nna comes back, because he wants it so."

Aku-nna opened her mouth and closed it again. Her Nna had told her that he was only staying there for a few hours; he had told her to prepare his evening meal because he would be back by the time the sun went down. But Nna had never said a word about his pains — oh, but Nna had not told her many, many things. She felt betrayed. Why, oh, why did he tell Uncle Uche the truth and lie to her? She almost hated her two uncles for knowing what she did not know about her own family. What she still had to learn was the fact that her people, the people of Ibuza, have what psychologists would call the group mind. They all help each other when in trouble or in need, and the extended family system still applied even in a town like Lagos, hundreds of miles from Ibuza. They are a people who think alike, whose ways are alike, so much so that it would not occur to any one of them to behave and act differently. Even if Nna had not told his nephew Uche, it would have been Uche's responsibility to find out and to take care of his young cousins. That Aku-nna did not know was due to the fact that she was still a child, and her father suspected that she was growing into the type of young woman who would not only want to give everything to a person she loved but who would also worry over her loved ones. He did not want his

16

daughter to suffer or worry unduly. Aku-nna knew that there was a kind of bond between her and her father which did not exist between her and her mother. She loved her father, and he responded as much as their custom allowed — for was she not only a girl? A girl belonged to you today as your daughter, and tomorrow, before your very eyes, would go to another man in marriage. To such creatures, one should be wary of showing too much love and care, otherwise people would ask, "Look, man, are you going to be your daughter's husband as well?" Despite all that, Aku-nna knew she held a special place in her father's heart. She was not going to let these two uncles know how she felt, that she felt betrayed and that she was frightened for her father's feet, his health, his life. She put on a bold face, but her emotions showed in her large, wondering eyes; they were moist, tears were not far away.

It still surprised her, though, that Nna had arranged it so that Uche, who he said was lazy and as sluggish as a woman expecting twins, was to be trusted with his children. And Uche was complying, even though Nna had almost sliced off one of his ears when Uche had so annoyed him one day that Nna could not control his temper.

Aku-nna remembered that day well. Nna had come home for his midday meal and had seen Uche sitting on one of their chairs, with his hair and body well groomed and smelling of coconut oil. He sat there, Uncle Uche did, singing from the CMS hymn book. Nna had called him by name in a voice as rough as a motor engine gone rusty. At first Uche did not answer, and Nna went to drink from the glass placed ready for him on the food table. He called him again, this time in a voice as murderous as that of an angry lion caught in a hunter's trap. Uche jumped, and so did Aku-nna and her brother Nna-nndo who was standing by, hoping Nna would leave him a piece of meat as he usually did (for according to their custom no father should finish all the food on his plate: he must leave a piece of meat or fish for his children to share). On this day, Nna-nndo sensed trouble and moved further away, nearer the door. Then Nna spoke:

"What are you doing here, Uche-nna?" Uche-nna, meaning "father's thoughts", was Uncle Uche's full name, and when Nna called anybody by their full name it always spelt trouble. "What are you doing here?" he asked again, drawing closer, his eyes as red as palm fruits.

"Nothing, just singing," Uche had answered then, quivering like banana leaves caught in a terrible tornado.

"What do you mean, 'Nothing, just singing'?"

Before Uche could open his mouth to explain, Nna's drinking glass flew and crashed against the wall behind Uncle Uche. The children screamed, and an engine driver by the name of Abosi, an Ibo man from Owerri who like Nna was home for a midday meal, rushed into their room just in time to extract Uncle Uche from the scene. For Uche, too, was blinded by anger and was making for Nna like a mad bull.

"What are you going to do?" Abosi, who was a very tall man, demanded of Uche. "Fight your little father?" Among the Ibo people, an elderly male relative, who looks after you like a father, is referred to as your "big father" if he is older than your natal father. Nna was younger than Uche's father.

That very day Uche had left their house for good because Nna maintained that he could not stand layabouts.

As all these thoughts ran through Aku-nna's mind, she was sure Uche was going to avenge himself on her and her brother. But Uncle Uche's face did not look like that of a man set on revenge. He looked not only sorry but worried as well. When he spoke it was very, very slowly, in a voice that was thick and saddened, telling Aku-nna that going to a hospital did not mean death, that her father would come back to them in a day or two, that she was not to cry or be frightened at all, because there was nothing to be frightened about. Aku-nna was amazed; her Uncle Uche seemed to be suffering too, suffering for her father's sake.

The people of Ibuza have a proverb which says that quarrels between relatives are only skin deep; they never penetrate to the bones. They have another saying, that on the day of blood relatives, friends go. This day then was the day of blood relatives. Aku-nna was learning.

All that was three weeks ago, and still Nna had not arrived home from the hospital.

Ma Blackie had sent a telegram from Ibuza asking them to confirm the rumour she had heard that her husband was ill. Members of Nna's family in Lagos had decided against telling her the truth.

18

Through Nna Beaty, Beaty's mother, a friend of Ma Blackie's who happened to be going to Ibuza at the time, they told her not to worry, that her children were being well looked after, that her husband was only in hospital for a day or two and would be out very soon. She was strongly advised to direct her attention to the important work she had been sent home to do — to placate the goddess of the river Oboshi into giving her more sons and daughters. She was not to concern herself about her family in Lagos at all, for what was there to worry about? Was Uche not looking after her children for her? So Ma stayed at Ibuza.

"It is now exactly three weeks since Nna went to hospital," Aku-nna thought to herself, sitting on the mat spread on the ground in the back yard. She did not know for sure who had spread that mat there — maybe it was Ndidi's mother or Azuka's mother — but as the mat was clean and nobody was sitting there, she sat on it, cross-legged, as well brought up girls were supposed to sit. You are taught from childhood that when you sit you must make the cloth of your lappa, called *iro* in Yoruba, into a kite-like shape, so that a point of it goes between your legs, to cover your sex. The crossing of the legs was added as a double security, just in case the kite effect had not achieved the desired result; when a girl sat with her legs crossed, it served to ward off the curious and prying gazes of young males.

Aku-nna watched the houseboys playing draughts. She wondered now when her father would be back, and when her mother would be back. For a while she had enjoyed the role of the little mistress of the house, but now she was fed up with it. She had reached the stage when she would give everything to come home from school and find her mother, Ma Blackie, sitting there on the veranda plaiting her long, black, shiny hair, telling her that they were having her favourite Agbona soup. Aku-nna loved that soup and would eat her utmost whenever Ma Blackie made it; agbona is a vegetable that draws like okro, and it made the swallowing of pounded yam very easy and tasted delicious. She longed, too, for the day she would again be able to run to meet her father as he came home from work, to feel his comfort when she complained that her mother had told her off or beaten her again. She wanted it all to be the way it used to be before. Everything seemed to have changed so much within just a month, she thought, except perhaps the sun and the moon and the stars. They remained the same, coming out or hiding behind clouds at their appropriate times.

On this particular afternoon, the round sun that was setting behind the kitchen in the back yard was fire-like in colour and intensity. The blue sky was patterned beautifully by white cotton-wool clouds, all fluffy with shapes uncertain. Long human shadows announced the approaching evening. From the nearby Loco yard came the penetrating sound of a siren, a gun was fired from somewhere in the docks, and everybody knew that it was four o'clock. Four o'clock was the time all manual workers went home. It was the time when all housewives stopped plaiting their hair, when they finished off their gossiping because their menfolk would soon be home, hungry, tired and irritable; so the women would rush to their kitchen to prepare the evening meal. Four o'clock was a very important hour in the lives of the families of men working at the Loco. At the house where Aku-nna and her parents lived, some houseboys had marked the sun's progress at four o'clock, just in case for some reason or other they missed the siren or the gun shot: at four, the sun, keeping regular hours in Africa near the equator, would rest on that line drawn with charcoal on the outside of the kitchen wall.

The hurry towards the kitchen had now begun. Housewives carried their blackened iron pots in one hand and the pieces of yam they were going to pound in their various odos in the other. The houseboys tightened their tattered shorts and left the draughts boards in haste to prepare food for their masters. Aku-nna sat there on the mat, watching them all as an outsider would — an outsider who wished to belong to the bustle and the urgency and yet could not, since there was nothing for her to rush for. She could not rush to the kitchen for her father, because Nna was not coming home at four; she could not hurry to cook for a husband because, though she was nearing fourteen, her father would not hear of her marrying early. So she sat there, without purpose, as if her life had come to an abrupt end.

Dick, one of the houseboys, darted her a strange, owl-like glance and looked away rather too quickly. Aku-nna wondered why, because the houseboys normally teased her until she was reduced to tears, but the look Dick had given her on his hasty way to the kitchen was full of sympathy. She tried to forget it, and her mind turned to the lots of the houseboys. Most Ibo "big men" in Lagos had started out as houseboys. Even her Nna had been a houseboy to a Bishop Onyeaboh; she had seen a picture of the godly bishop, smiling benignly in his black and white church robes. As a young man of fifteen or so, you would go to live with a bachelor relative, maybe an uncle or cousin. You would clean, cook and wash for him, and by way of payment you were fed, clothed in your master's cast-offs and, if you were lucky, would attend evening classes to learn a trade that would see you through life. The master would use this period of time to save for the price of the bride he would eventually marry, and to equip himself with furniture and clothes. In most cases, with the arrival of the bride there were clashes — the houseboy wanting to control the household and the bride wanting to do the same. The bride usually won, and then the houseboy would go away in search of his own fortune somewhere else. It was always so, and it still is so among the Ibos in Lagos today. It is one of those unwritten norms which are here to stay.

Unconsciously, Aku-nna checked the kitchen wall, to see whether the sun had made a mistake for once, but it had not. The reflection rested perfectly on the charcoaled line. Suddenly the shrill voice of her Aunt Uzo jarred into her thoughts.

"Aku-nna. . . . Aku-nna, ooooo. . . ."

"Yes, Auntie!" she shouted back, scrambling to her feet and turning to the direction from where the call came. She saw her aunt approaching. "Have you been looking for me? I was just sitting here," Aku-nna's voice sounded apologetic, "doing nothing."

Auntie Uzo came nearer and greeted her quietly. "I am glad I have been able to find you at last." She looked tired, as if the hot sun had squeezed the very juice of life from her.

Aku-nna's gaze wandered to the sturdy boy baby Uzo carried at her side. He was dipping his fat hands into his mother's loose Nigerian blouse, searching out her breasts. The blouse was obviously obstructing his movements, for he pushed his woolly head under it as well, and eventually caught one breast with his hungry mouth. Uzo, to help him, folded her blouse up to her neck and gave him a pendulous right breast. This time the baby took it properly and started to suck greedily, shaking his fat feet to the rhythm of his enjoyment, bouncing up and down in playful wildness. A little of the milk that gushed down his throat escaped from the corners of his mouth and trickled down to the folds of fatty flesh around his neck. Uzo looked at her baby and then conspiratorially at Aku-nna, and they both smiled almost simultaneously.

The spontaneous smile took the tiredness off Auntie Uzo's face, so that for that brief moment it was wrinkle-less. Then as suddenly as the smile had appeared, it disappeared again, and her face assumed its usual narrow look. Not that Auntie Uzo was an old woman; she was in fact very young, and baby Okechukwu was her first. Nobody knew for sure, though, exactly when Uzo had been born but, as the baby was eighteen months old, she was probably between the ages of sixteen and eighteen or nineteen. She had been brought to Lagos from Ibuza to be married to her husband, Dogo. "Dogo" is a nickname given by the Hausas to any tall person. Uzo's Dogo had been a driver in the army during the war against Hitler, so had come into contact with lots of Hausas. When the war was over, he wanted to marry a wife with the army money he had received, and Aku-nna's father had told him: "My cousin's daughter is grown now. She comes from a very tall family too, so why don't you pay for her? She will give you tall sons, because her father was tall and her mother, who is still alive, is also tall." Dogo liked Uzo and Dogo paid for Uzo, and Nna helped them to get a room in Akinwunmi Street and now they had this fat, greedy baby who was eating Auntie Uzo up, making her look too old for her age, making her dry, giving her the appearance of a female giant.

"Tonight I am going to tell you a story which I've just heard from a friend who arrived from home yesterday," Uzo said. "Actually, I knew the story before but I had forgotten it, and I don't think I have told it to you and Nna-nndo before. This particular one is very long and has two lovely songs in it — the kind of songs you like. So you'd better hurry and do your cooking now," Auntie Uzo finished, as she swung her baby to the other breast. Then all of a sudden she cried out in pain, "You wicked child! I have never in all my life come across a child as thoughtless as you are. You keep chewing my nipples as if they are chewing sticks. Don't you know that they hurt? Do you want to bite them off? You are not the only child I am going to have, you know. Others will come, and I shall need my nipples to feed them with. If you bite me like that again, I shall give you a spank."

Amused, Aku-nna watched Uzo and her baby. So did Azuka's mother, who was on her way to the kitchen. "You are not expecting another one yet, are you?" the latter asked, rather seriously.

"What a nasty thing to say," replied Uzo. "And on a day like this, too. He is only eighteen months old; he is much too young to be weaned."

The smile evaporated from Azuka's mother's face, and she walked determinedly towards the kitchen. She called back to Aku-nna, "Come and cook your evening meal."

Aku-nna was taken aback by this urgency. Why was it everyone was so concerned about her cooking? And what did Uzo mean when she said to Azuka's mother "on a day like this"? What was wrong with the day, she wondered? She had been to school as usual, the sun had shone as usual, and now the sun was going down as usual. So what was suddenly so remarkable? She peered at Auntie Uzo's face, but was greeted by a look as blank as any plain paper. There was no clue as to what the two women were secretly referring. So she shrugged her shoulders and hurried to do as she was told.

Aku-nna liked listening to Auntie Uzo's stories, for she was a born storyteller. Aku-nna, like most of her friends, had been born in Lagos, but her parents and relatives were fond of telling nostalgic stories about their town Ibuza. Most of the stories were like fairytales but with the difference that nearly all used the typical African call-and-response songs: the storyteller would call, and all the listeners would respond. Auntie Uzo was particularly gifted in the art of these songs. Sometimes her voice would rise, clean and clear, ringing like the sound of a thousand tiny bells. And when the story was a sad one, her call would be low, still clear but sounding like an angry stream rushing down a fall. This type of song was often so moving that tears would well up in the eyes of her audience. Invariably Uzo would ask the listeners to make rhythmic heavy groans, in imitation of the sounds produced by the master drummers in the remote villages around Ibuza. In between the pulsating groans and the mournful song would be repeated refrains, at first in high and then in descending pitches. And the listeners would be awe-struck to silence, their terrified minds imagining many things.

The stories were so intensely charged with philosophical lessons about one thing or another that Aku-nna and her friends were able to learn from them. What attracted her most, though, were the whoops and calls about the life of her ancestors. They had been real forest people, whose births, marriages and deaths were celebrated alike with wild dances of coal-black maidens wearing short raffia skirts, performing the *aja* or *oduko* with bells on their thin ankles. Their bare tops were beautified with black leafy tattoos, and their laughter was loud and elaborate. There were lots of witch doctors, too, with heads shaved so closely that they looked like skeleton skulls. . . .

Remembering that Auntie Uzo had promised another story, Aku-nna was eager to get on with her cooking. But the idiotic fire would not start. She knelt on the kitchen floor and puffed at the stubborn sparks, and all they did was to glow and then go dead. The fire just would not start. Instead, the smoke went into her eyes and, as she tried to cough, she swallowed a mouthful of it, as old women do when smoking their clay pipes. But she was not smoking any pipe, and she did not want the hurting smoke in her lungs. Her cough increased, and Alice asked her if she was all right. Although she insisted that she was, Alice, looking more serious than she normally was, lit the fire for her and then continued peeling her yam. Alice was a new bride, and like Aku-nna she was almost fourteen; her husband worked as a clerk at the Treasury. Aku-nna thanked her. But she was aware that everybody was unusually subdued, cooking quickly as if they were anxious to leave the kitchen as soon as possible.

It was a large room with a chimney corner on one side, and it served as kitchen for all the occupants of the sixteen-roomed house in Akinwunmi Street, Yaba, where Aku-nna lived. It was now thick with the smoke escaping from the sixteen or so earthenware cooking stoves ranged round the walls. The chimney was incapable of drawing the smoke from all of the fires, so smoke just rose and curled round and round the ceiling. Sometimes it would be so dense that one would swear that the chimney was emitting smoke instead of sucking it up. In the kitchen, your eyes watered and your nose ran in sympathy. Each stove was moulded with an open front, into which long pieces of firewood were shoved; the firewood was lighted, and earthenware cooking pots were placed on top of the burning wood, which had to be tended and poked every so often, so that the fire burned brighter and fiercer until the food in the pot was cooked. When you walked into the kitchen you saw what looked like square portions of fire along the walls, with each cook huddling on the cemented floor in front of a square of fire, either poking it, or stirring the food, or peeling a piece of yam, or simply wiping a teary eye or a clammy nose. One or two cooks might have nothing to do but watch their fires burn and sing some tune, mostly wordless and out of key.

But this afternoon, even the houseboy Dick did not sing his usual "Killy me die o Abana". He too was quiet, his tongue as ever hanging at one side of his mouth but his sharp black eyes untypically soft. He pointed out to Aku-nna that her fire had gone out again.

"The wood you are using is not properly dried," he explained. "That is why it causes so much smoke and will not burn easily. Here, move your pot onto my own stove. I have finished now."

Aku-nna was overwhelmed. She had never dreamed that Dick was capable of so much goodness. She vowed silently never again to call him "Snake Tongue" — a nickname Dick rightly hated, even though it suited him so. After all, she reasoned within herself, Dick could not help the way he was made. He could not help licking the soup-spoon with his narrow tongue the way he did, darting it here and there, and in the process making sibilant sounds so like a hissing snake; nor could he help having a mouth so small and so bird-like that it reminded people more of the pointed beak of a hungry vulture than of a feature of any human living. God had given him these peculiarities. All Dick had done was to accept them, because there was nothing he could do about them. So Aku-nna forgave him and, by way of encouragement, enthused to him:

"Auntie Uzo is going to tell us one of her stories this evening, by the electric pole. I am sure she won't mind if you join us."

Dick gave her one of his snake-like glances and said, in tones so low they sounded like the noise made by a man being strangled, "I know about the story. I shall be sitting there listening by the electric pole." He went quiet again, as though he was thinking. Then he added, louder than before, as if it were an afterthought, "I like the Asaba folk-songs a lot." Dick was also an Ibo, but from the eastern side of the River Niger. The Ibos from that part generally refer to their brothers west of the Niger as "the people from Asaba" — Asaba is a great Ibo trading town on the west

25

of the river, a very old and a very historic town.

Gloom seemed to have descended from somewhere onto everybody in the kitchen. Aku-nna could feel it but she had stopped wondering about it. Now she hurried to escape from it all. She was grateful that she only had to warm up their two-day old soup, to pound a small portion of yam for herself and her brother. It would not matter too much if the pounded yam turned out lumpy, nor would it matter if it turned out hard. She and her brother were not that fussy. All that mattered was that the yam should be cooked and pounded, that was all they wanted, and she intended to make it as quickly as she could.

Soon she had finished. Her eyes were red and her chest was wheezing with the smoke. She clambered up from her huddled posture, wiped her damp hands on her house lappa with the fish pattern on it, and walked out into the yard, as it were into freedom. She carried the pounded yam on her head and walked proudly, stopping at the steps leading into the house and looking round to see if she could find her brother to call him inside to eat. Nna-nndo, however, like all boys of his age, was busy playing in unthinkable places.

Aku-nna saw that the sun was not setting very fast. It had turned a deep red, like a ball of flame, and its edges were neater and sharper. It seemed to be suspended there in the heavens, among the clouds, by strings that were invisible to any human eye. The fiery heat it had been sending out earlier in the day was gone, and now its rays were gentle, caressing, like the touch of a tender mother.

Aku-nna sighed and went inside.

Surprisingly, Auntie Uzo was already in the room. She was not sitting down but stood looking out of their only window onto the yard. Aku-nna did not ask her how she came to be there, because most of the tenants seldom locked their doors, but kept them open to allow in the cool evening air. Uzo turned round, firmly, as if tugged by a rope. Her attitude was exceptionally gentle. It seemed that she stooped, that the weight of her lolling breasts — breasts full of baby Okechukwu's milk — was pulling her down. Her eyes were still troubled, and Aku-nna was sure that she had been crying. She wanted to ask why Auntie Uzo was not holding her baby, why her eyes were red, why she had been so keen that Aku-nna make the evening meal. Aku-nna was prevented from asking, because in her culture it would have been bad manners, and if so many questions had come from a young girl like herself it would have been considered even worse than bad manners.

Uzo looked at her long and hard, then all at once seemed to collect herself. "I thought I told you to hurry, that I wanted to tell you a story this evening," she said in her usual admonishing voice.

"But I did hurry. I've looked everywhere for Nna-nndo but I can't find him."

"Don't worry about Nna-nndo. Just eat your share. He will come in when he is hungry. He always does."

So encouraged, Aku-nna washed her hands in the bowl of water she had provided for herself, took her portion of the pounded yam and began to roll it into balls small enough to pass through her throat. She had soon had her fill. So she ate the piece of stock-fish in her soup bowl, and lapped up the rest of the soup, making much noise in her haste, for she could sense the urgency in Uzo's mood, as Uzo gazed vacantly out of the window. Aku-nna sucked her fingers rapidly, picked up the bowls from the floor and made for the food cabinet.

She was stopped by a loud knock on the door. Aku-nna peeped through the curtain and she saw, standing there in the doorway, another aunt, this one older and skinnier and with the name of Mary. Auntie Mary stood there holding Nna-nndo by the wrist, and she too was looking very unhappy. Aku-nna was now frightened. She dropped the bowls with a clatter, and allowed her eyes to notice the hurriedly tied lappa round Auntie Mary's waist. Auntie Mary, another close relative of Nna, was a very fashion-conscious woman; she seldom visited them because she lived a long way away at Ebute-Metta. The thought flashed through Aku-nna's head that something must be drastically wrong for her to come to see them like this, looking so rough. She made to look from one aunt to the other to learn what was lurking behind their red eyes.

Then another visitor entered, this time a man, one of the most respected men in Ibuza. Some people said he was a doctor: he looked well-fed, well groomed and he spoke in a voice that was always low, just like real doctors in hospitals do. He wore glasses too, glasses that were gold-rimmed and were always shining. But although Mazi Arinze worked at the General Hospital in Lagos island, he was only a dispenser. It was beyond the reach of many

Ibuza families to afford any other doctor, so Mazi Arinze became everybody's doctor. He could cure anything, from gaping yaws to snake bites; even sleeping sickness and malaria were not too much for him. He specialised in all. His charges were reasonable. Nna had said that with Arinze you only had to pay for the drugs — though nobody knew where he got the drugs from, whether they had been prescribed for hospital patients or whether they were drugs belonging to the hospital. It did not matter much where the drugs came from. According to a Yoruba saying, if you work by the altar you must eat from the altar; you are a wicked man if you refuse to give it up when your time is up. So Arinze was not acting without the common accord. He was simply conforming to another of the unwritten laws of the children of the Niger.

This Arinze now stood solidly by the doorway, with lowered eyes. Then Aku-nna and her brother knew the reason for the sudden visits of their relatives, then they acknowledged the message behind the swollen eyes of Auntie Uzo and Auntie Mary. Then they knew what had happened. Nna had died.

Aku-nna felt as if she was not there, as if she had passed into that realm where nothing exists. At last her brother's voice — young, immature, boyish — cut through to her, sharply painful like the slash of a razor blade.

"We have no father anymore. There is no longer any schooling for me. This is the end."

But, Nna-nndo, you have got it all wrong, Aku-nna said to herself. It is not that we have no father any more, we have no parents any more. Did not our father rightly call you Nna-nndo, meaning "Father is the shelter"? So not only have we lost a father, we have lost our life, our shelter!

It is so even today in Nigeria: when you have lost your father, you have lost your parents. Your mother is only a woman, and women are supposed to be boneless. A fatherless family is a family without a head, a family without shelter, a family without parents, in fact a non-existing family. Such traditions do not change very much.

28

3

The Burial

Ezekiel Odia's funeral was, like all such ceremonies in colonial Africa, a mixture of the traditional and the European. Emphasis was always placed on the European aspect. The European ways were considered modern, the African old-fashioned. Lagos culture was such an unfortunate conglomeration of both that you ended up not knowing to which you belonged.

In his lifetime, Ezekiel was a typical product of this cultural mix. He would preach the Gospel on Sundays, he would sing praises to the European Living God, he would force his children to pray every morning, to pray before and after meals; but all this did not prevent him calling in a native medicine-man when the occasion arose. In fact, behind his door there was a gourd containing a magical potion which served as protection for the family; a man must not leave his family unprotected. The gourd was well hidden, out of sight behind the church wedding photograph of him and his wife Ma Blackie. He was buried in the same way that he had lived: in a conflict of two cultures.

At the first announcement of his death, the traditional crying began. This was an art in itself. There were expert professional criers, who listed the good deeds performed by the departed and tactfully left out the bad. His lineage would be traced out loud, the victories of his ancestors sung and their heroic past raised to the winds, amidst the groans of other criers, the screams of women and the heart beats of the men. Such force was put into these cries. The first storm of them rose like an angry thunder, in different deafening pitches. The high, penetrating shrieks of the women somehow managed to have a touch of apathy in them, as if their voices were saying: "We do our share of the crying because it is expected of us, but what can one do when faced with death? It is a call we must all answer, however busy we are." Their noises of protest against death were followed by pathetic low howls, like those of a slave who knows he is to be sacrificed for the life of his sick master. The men's howlings were of a lower key, charged with energy and producing sounds that resembled the growls of hundreds of angered lions. They beat their chests to the rhythm of their agony, they hugged themselves this way and that like raging waves on a gloomy day, and on each face ran two rivers of tears which looked as though they would never dry.

Aku-nna and Nna-nndo were the chief mourners. Their cries of grief were expected to be more convincing than those of the others, for was it not their father who had died? Their own cries must be made in the most artistic way, because one loses one's father only once. Aku-nna had seen her mother cry at the deaths of relatives, and had heard stories of how relatives mourn their lost loved ones. She did not know her father's genealogical tree in detail, so she sang out only of what she knew.

"My father was a good provider. My father was a good Christian. He was a good husband to my mother Ma Blackie. He bought me many dresses. He spoilt me. He sent me to school." This was followed by a long cry of pained sorrow, wordless but moving.

Then: "Who will spoil me now? Who will send me to school? Who will feed me? Who will be a good husband to Nne? Nne, my mother . . . where are you? Come back from Ibuza for you have lost your husband, the husband who married you according to our custom and again married you in the church. . . . Come back, for you have lost the father of your children. . . ."

On and on went Aku-nna, repeating her father's attributes. She did not stop, not even when the other mourners became more subdued. Nobody could stop her, for this was what was expected of a daughter. People later remarked that for a girl not born in Ibuza she did not do too badly.

Nna-nndo did not use many words. He simply howled and threw himself about. Grown-up men held him tight, so that he did not hurt himself. He soon finished crying, but Aku-nna was encouraged to continue; girls were supposed to exhibit more emotion.

By this time the room was filled with people. The tenants, the houseboys, the relatives, tens and tens of them poured in from all parts of Lagos. Everyone wept their fill. Each new mourner would come, take a look at the two young children, listen for a second to Aku-nna's cry, then go out onto the veranda and start to wail. They all knew that this would happen to them one day, in turns. A death like this could happen in their own family; in fact they could be the next victim. So they cried, not just for Ezekiel Odia's young children, or for Ezekiel, but for themselves.

The early shock began to lessen. Criers were becoming exhausted. There were still occasional moans and sad outbursts as each new relative arrived. Aku-nna persisted in her cries, but their impact was ebbing. To many of the people sitting there, heads listlessly hanging, Ezekiel Odia had gone to meet his ancestors. He was dead.

One by one, as if compelled by a force felt only by them, the men started to move towards the front of the house, into the open air. The moon was up and full, but its brilliance was put to shame by the stronger light provided by the electric pole outside the house in Akinwunmi Street. It was such a hot night that the men stripped off their upper garments; some who wore lappa cloths wrapped round themselves left those, some were now only in their shorts. They then linked hands to form a big circle and began to stamp and move, first to one side then to the other. This wordless movement of about fifty strong men, in their prime of life, lasted for a minute or two. Then all of a sudden there was a call, near and yet distant — the heavy movements made it hard to know from where it came. A solo singer took up the call. He was calling Death, telling him to wake up, to see what he had done. Had he not taken Ezekiel from among them? He had made it impossible for Ezekiel to know the whereabouts of his son. He had snatched Ezekiel away before he had time to enjoy the bride price his daughter would fetch. Death had taken Ezekiel away, for ever and ever!

While the soloist catalogued all that Death had done to Ezekiel and his family, the other men, now turned wild dancers — still moving in their circle, hands now held tighter than before, feet beating the parched, sun-baked soil — suddenly all together let out a great whoop. Then they whirled faster and faster, thickening the air with awakened dust, singing strangely and wildly. They sweated profusely and their coal-black bodies shone in the light.

As the intensity of the dance rose, the women, tears still welling in their eyes, started to filter out to join their menfolk. Soon the circle had become so large that it had to be broken into smaller

31

circles. It was now the women who took up the calls. The men had done their part; they had awakened Death, from where he was reposing in the land of the departed. It was now for the women to sing Ezekiel's way to death, paving the path with their bell-like voices so that his journey would be smooth and without hitch. The sounds that rose from them were moving, purposely prolonged but full of words sung so rapidly that, to the untutored ear, they would be compared to the noise made when a bricklayer pours little pebbles on a zinc roof. Yet despite this effect, one could not help being carried away by the smoothness that linked the words together in a tanquil, undisturbed stream. The men replied to the continuing chant in low voices, and theirs were like the sighs of men who, though defeated, have never let go of their dignity.

Then the death dance took another turn. Gourds laced with beads and cowries were produced. Hands unclasped, and the women were each given a gourd. The songs still continued, many different ones, with varied tunes and twists, the legacy of an ancient culture. To these were now added the shaking of the beaded gourds, producing a samba-like but very African sound. The motion of the circle had losts its frenziedness, and the concentration was on the women's singing and rattling of the gourds, the clapping of the men's hands. But if the wildness had gone from the group, it was reappearing in solo dancers. One or two would jump into the centre of the circle, to fast clapping and gourd-shaking and even louder calls, and like mad Christians gone berserk would roll themselves into balls, then uncurl again, working their bodies into lumpy or smooth shapes, like a huge dough being prepared for pastry. The dancers would first hold their hands close to their chests, then wave them high as if imitating the wings of angels, then back to their chests, stamping their feet rhythmically in response to changes in the clapping, chanting and gourd-shaking. When the song rose, the dancer's limbs moved more fiercely, the very earth seemed roused by the heavy stamping; when the song ebbed into a chorus, the dancer clasped his chest, becoming lithe and graceful as a cat at play. As the chants went up and down, so did the dancer's hands. The whole atmosphere was a harmonious mass of rises and falls.

The falls in intensity became prolonged as people tired. Kegs of palm wine were bought and handed round. Plates of kolanuts were distributed.

During a particularly long lull, another singing was heard from the next compound. Those were Christian hymns and, though sung in Ibo to a heavily Africanised beat, they still had far to go before they could compete with the traditional death songs. The Christians sang their songs about a New Jerusalem, occasionally sounding completely out of tune as the effect of the palm wine took hold.

All night it went on. The crying of the close relatives inside the room, the hot, native songs of the mourners outside, and the slower, stranger Christian strains. The air was filled with the combined din of the three groups, and so confused and noisy was it that many a time you could not tell which sound emanated from which direction.

The moon disappeared. The bright night gradually gave way to a grey, damp morning; mist was everywhere and dew formed tiny silvery drops behind the leaves of the lemon grass that grew wild in front of the house. Here, an exhausted mourner was lying down, his naked body pulsating in the aftermath of the night's hullabaloo; there, another old one was stretched out on a bench, like a dead man himself, his laboured breath quavering, wheezing out of his wrinkled hairless chest. The compound, the adjacent compound and the one next to that looked like deserted battlefields; the ground was so trodden that, with the early morning dampness, the normally hidden red mud had come to the surface. Chairs, hired from professional lenders for a shilling a dozen, and benches, borrowed from a teacher of private students, were strewn all over the place, like the swords and shields of the Zulu warriors after one of their numerous defeats by British soldiers with superior arms.

Then a cock crowed, and it was time to go. The wake was over. An uncle of the children got up from the cool cement where he had been lying, stretched expansively, letting out a loud, salivary yawn as he did so, and said under his breath:

"Trust the cocks to start crowing just when I was beginning to enjoy my sleep. Still, no matter. I must go and get permission for absence from my work." Then he remembered that today was Saturday, and he smiled. Fancy a quiet man like Ezekiel dying on a Friday, so that he might be buried on a Saturday, a day most convenient for funerals. It was going to be a big procession, for all the workers would be free to come.

33

Aku-nna had not slept much. Their room was filled with so many people; women with bodies shiny from sweat lay in a neat row on the mat spread on the cool floor. She had been sandwiched between a cousin, who scratched all night because she had craw-craw, and another very large woman whose heavy bosom rose and fell with her breathing, like that of an angry hippopotamus. Aku-nna sat up and stretched, and tried to work out how she was related to this woman, whom her mother usually referred to as her sister Matilda (pronounced "Matinda"). In Ibuza, relationships were so vague and complicated that it was always easier to pronounce every close relative "see-se-ta" or "buu-lo-da", though Aku-nna was sure that this woman could not be a real sister of her mother's. She soon stopped wondering about it, for another sound attracted her attention.

It came from Autie Uzo and her baby. Auntie Uzo's breathing was gentle, like the sighing of a small stream flowing through some bushes. She was so thin, yet so supple that the arm she put round her baby was like a young snake lying peaceably, gleaming, black and smooth. Baby Okechukwu was fast asleep but his sleepy mouth was plugged by Uzo's heavy nipple. He tugged dozily at his mother's breast, making funny animal grunts, like a little puppy, as his throat received the milk. Aku-nna smiled, despite herself.

She stood up, feeling a need to go to the back yard. She had to be very careful not to tread on those still sleeping. Uncle Richard's body was lying right there across the doorway, his hands clasped to his chest as if he were a man of God saying a benediction; he had only four fingers on one of his hands, the result of an accident at his place of work. He was a born moaner — not that he had nothing to moan about, for his lot in life was very sad. Like Nna, he too had gone to the war, though no one knew for sure whether he had ever left North Africa or seen any action. But he told many stories of his exploits, of his experiencies in Japan, in Burma, in India. How could Uncle Richard have been to all those places in one war, especially since as everyone knew he had had very little education? He would go into gory details of how the Japanese trapped and killed many British soldiers. The Japanese would leave expensive wrist-watches lying about, he once told Aku-nna and her brother, and if you happened to come from a culture which did not teach you that you must not steal, as soon as you touched the watches you would get your head blown to pieces. It was Uncle Richard who had told the children what had happened to Nna's feet, giving such an elaborate description that you would have thought that he had actually been there, in the same regiment. However Nna was conscripted two years before Uncle Richard went, and the latter did not stay all that long before the end of the war. He claimed that his regiment saw Hitler die, slowly by poison, crying like a woman in labour pains for the gods of the German people to help him. He was a good storyteller, Uncle Richard; maybe that was why he had been put in uniform in the first place — to amuse his fellow soldiers.

But now his stories had bitter edges in them, not very amusing any longer. Things had happened to him to make him lose his sense of humour. First he had started losing his front teeth; he lost four altogether, all at the top of his mouth, and the two teeth on either side of the gap were still so white and so pointed that they gave his face the look of a black crocodile. Then he lost a finger; the pain this lost middle finger gave him never ceased to fascinate him. He would itemise for you every groan it had ever caused him to groan, and would moan about how life had never been the same since. He would cry, "To think I went to fight a monster in human form like Hitler and survived with all my fingers, only to come back and lose one here in my own country, among my own people, when I was simply sawing wood!" His listeners would pity and shake their heads, agreeing that life is a sad and cruel business. Even though Uncle Richard had only spent a few months in the army, they paid him a lot of money after his discharge. He spent it wisely, and married himself a wife by the name of Rebecca. She was a very quiet girl, a little on the plump side but too beautiful, too young for Uncle Richard. He never stopped beating her because he said Rebecca was always making eyes at other men. They would come from their house in the island to state their cases to Nna and Ma Blackie. Richard invariably lost the cases, and Nna kept warning him that, if he did not stop ill-treating his wife, he would soon lose her too. That was exactly what happened. And to cap it all, he carried his bitterness to his work and they soon sacked him, because they said he did not try to get on with his mates. So Uncle Richard was jobless, wifeless, with missing teeth and finger, but Nna had always made certain that at least he had a full belly whenever he came to visit them, which was quite often.

Aku-nna was contemplating how she would make a big jump across the sleeping body without hurting the offended hand, especially as that very hand lay uppermost on his chest, the mutilation now more grotesque in the dim light so that she did not want to have to look at it again. She heaved, lifted her little self up and leaped. She did not fall on Uncle Richard, but she startled him into wakefulness.

"Oh, is it you?" he asked in his old, unsteady voice. Then he smiled sadly, unconsciously rubbing the swollen gap in his hand, his mouth displaying the wider gap among his teeth. This further look at the man shook Aku-nna into giving him his customary greeting. Every Ibuza person, with the exception of slaves and the children of slaves, was addressed with particular names of praise in a special greeting. Uncle Richard's greeting was the same as her father's, since their great-grandfathers were of the same parents: *Odozi ani*, which meant literally "beautifier of the land" but also had the sense of "bringer of peace".

"*Odozi ani*," was what Aku-nna wanted to say, as she was about to dash for the back yard. But to her surprise she realised that no sound was forthcoming. Try as hard as she might, all she was able to produce by way of noise was like that made by ageing frogs at the sides of marshy streams. It then dawned on her that she had lost her voice. What was she now going to use in her farewell cry for her father that evening at the burial itself? This worried her the more as she found that each new attempt to force herself to talk was not only useless but painful.

Noting this, Uncle Richard said, with the morning saliva bubbling from his quavering lips, "When the sun comes out, you must ask your little mother to buy you some bananas. They will clear your throat for you. You must cry a farewell cry for your father. You are his only daughter from his loins."

Aku-nna understood what old Uncle Richard meant. To the Ibos and some Yorubas in Nigeria, a natural mother is not a child's only mother. A grandmother may be known as the "big mother" or the "old mother", and one's actual mother may be called "little mother", if her mother or mother-in-law is still alive. The title is extended to all young aunts or elder sisters, in fact to any young female who helps in mothering the child. Ibuza is a town

36

where everybody knows everybody else, so a child ends up having so many mothers, so many fathers, that in some cases the child may not see much of his true parents. This is much encouraged because not only does the child grow up knowing many people and thinking well of them but also the natal parents' tendency to spoil their offspring is counteracted. It is very important that a child is the child of the community. So, Aku-nna knew that Uncle Richard was referring to Auntie Uzo.

Like the front of the house, the back yard resembled another battlefield. The freshness of the early morning air was not enough to camouflage the stench of urine, the heavy smell of left-over palm wine, the odour oozing from the open gutter where without doubt one or two mourners had relieved themselves of some intoxicants. Though most of the tenants were still asleep and though the night soil-man had emptied the pail of human droppings the night before, yet it was already half-full again. Aku-nna hurried, for she did not wish to tarry there longer than was necessary.

At the other end of the yard stood some giant earthenware pots. One of the pots was theirs, and it was Aku-nna's task to fill it with water every evening after the meal so that Nna could wash himself before leaving for work in the Loco yard in the mornings. She knew that she had not filled the water pot because of the happenings of the night before. Yet when she lifted the tin cover she was not surprised to find it filled with nice cool water. One of their neighbours must have done it; she wondered who. Since the announcement of her father's death, she had never stopped marvelling at the unwritten ways of her people. Then the realisation came to her again, now with even greater pain, that they would never see their father alive again, and she faced the shocking reality that his death would change her whole life. This time she could not shout her agony, for she had no voice, and this new sorrow hung on her chest with the heaviness she used to feel when carrying a load of firewood. Tears would not even come, though she felt that her heart was shedding enough tears to add to the weight of the heavy pain. Still, she used some water from the pot to wash her face and mouth, and the tang of the water, coupled with the cool dampness of the morning, seemed to revive her somewhat. She walked slowly to the front of the house and stood silently by the gate of the yard. It was

37

then that she saw many of her relatives, most of them men, rushing home. She stood there for quite a long time.

Inside the room people had begun to wake up, and there were bustling activities all over the place. Men hurried to the back yard to the fast-filling pail. Women held their young children over the gutter that ran at the side of the yard to wash their faces and clean their teeth. Life was beginning to continue.

"Aku-nna! Aku-nna, oooo!"

Aku-nna was startled and set out in the direction of the voice. She could not answer her usual "Eh!" because her painful throat would not comply. So she moved very fast, tightening her lappa round her young waist as she went. She recognised the voices of her little mothers calling her, and ran to them.

"Where were you?" Auntie Matilda wanted to know.

Aku-nna pointed to where she had been standing, since she could not speak, and the heaviness in her breast-less chest made her feel like the goddess in one of the rivers around Onitsha who is said to have breasts as large as huge pumpkins. The sensation was so real to her that she now clutched the flimsy nylon blouse she was wearing, her fingers tightening it around her throat as if that would relieve some of the pain.

"Are you cold then?" Uzo asked, her voice croaky from the songs and cries of the night before.

Aku-nna shook her head.

"Then leave your blouse alone. Do you want to tear it? Can't you see that you have no father any more? You are an orphan now, and you have to learn to take care of whatever clothes you have. Nobody is going to buy you any more, until you marry. Then your husband will take care of you."

"The pity of it all," put in Auntie Matilda, "is that they will marry her off very quickly in order to get enough money to pay Nna-nndo's school fees."

"Oh, that should not be difficult. She is not ugly, and not a crying beauty either, but she is soft, quiet and intelligent. She will gladden the heart of an educated man, you mark my words. Most girls from Lagos are very quickly married away to rich and educated men because of their smooth bodies and their schooling," explained Uzo.

"That is so," agreed Matilda. "You talk of smooth bodies — from where would they get the scars and scratches we had? Do

38

children born here in Lagos know what it is to uproot a strong cassava from parched and unwilling earth, only to find a large snake curled at the top of the plant watching their progress? Oh, no, the girls born nowadays have it all made for them. They are lucky. Why would they not have smooth bodies and supple forms?" She finished with a sigh. Then, as an afterthought, she added, turning to face Aku-nna direct: "This is the fate of us women. There is nothing we can do about it. We just have to learn to accept it."

Aku-nna was sure they were saying all this by way of consolation and also to prepare her for what was coming. They had tried to do so, but they had not succeeded. If anything, they had intensified her fear of the unknown. What was her fate going to be, she wondered?

When the sun came out, and the mist was fast drying from the wet leaves, the bean-sellers started to walk up and down the street, carrying the steaming cooked beans on their heads. Food sellers were everywhere hawking their stuff. A few houses further down the road, the rice-seller was announcing to everybody that her rice was cooked.

"What do you want for breakfast this morning?" Uzo asked.

Aku-nna did not know what she wanted, but she implied that she would like to know where her brother was.

"Oh," said Uzo, "he is staying with Mama John Bull."

Aku-nna immediately stopped worrying about her brother, for she knew that he would be well fed and cared for. Mama John Bull, who lived down the road, was a fat woman with fat children of her own — in Lagos all fat boy babies are called John Bull, thus her name indicated that she was John Bull's mother — and she felt it her duty to feed everyone until they became fat like all the members of her household. Mama John Bull's husband was related to Ma Blackie, so Nna-nndo was staying with family.

"If you don't want anything else to eat, then I will get you some bananas for your voice. Mine hurts me too this morning, so I should have some as well," Uzo said as she hurried off to the calls of her baby.

The rest of the day was a nightmare. People came and went. As noon approached the sun became hot, and people who came then stayed. Chairs were set out once more, songs were restarted exactly as before, people started to cry again, especially those who had not been present the night before. By two in the afternoon, even Aku-nna's voice returned, and the trampling had become intense. Her brother, by now washed and fed, sat alone on one of the benches, staring with fear at everyone who came or went. Somebody's voice cut through the din: "I wish the children's mother was here. They look so lost."

They did not just look lost, they felt lost. Suddenly a loud clamour came from the outside. The dancers stopped dancing, the Christians stopped singing. Everyone began to shout and scream — women placed their hands on their heads and screamed, men beat their chests and howled. Auntie Uzo held Aku-nna tight screaming, screaming, her closed eyes sending down tears as heavy as rain. Uncle Uche held Nna-nndo and was howling and shaking his head from side to side. Why this fresh outburst of emotion, the children wondered, startled?

Then Aku-nna realised that Uzo was screaming words into her ears. The noise was so deafening that it had not registered at first.

"Cry!" Uzo screamed. "Cry, for our father who went to the hospital a few weeks ago is now back. He is back! He is back! Our father is back! Ma Blackie, come and welcome your husband who went to hospital a few weeks ago, for he is back to bid you his final goodbye."

The fact then sank in to the children. Their father's body had been brought home. Aku-nna and her brother were marshalled into another room belonging to a neighbour. They were to stay there until their father's body was ready for them to see.

There was a long argument as to which group of privileged mourners would sit next to Nna's body. Nna was a pagan first, then a Christian, then a Christian and a pagan; so it was difficult to predict where exactly he was going after death. The Christians insisted that he would go to heaven in the clouds, among the angels at the right hand of the living God, because he had never missed church, he had been a good tenor singer and he had lived a moderate life, offending no one. A quiet man. The Ibuza mourners said Nna was the son of a great oracle diviner. They were sure his father was there in the earth *"ani nmo"*, waiting for his son. So they were going to dance him down to hell.

Eleven-year-old Nna-nndo had somehow become wiser and older since his father's death. They called upon him to decide.

Old Uncle Richard, steaming with anger, dragged Nna-nndo from where he was sitting and, wagging his swollen four-fingered hand at him, appealed.

"You know," he started, his missing teeth making it almost impossible for his hearers to make out what it was he was trying to say; the problem was worsened by the fact that Uncle Richard's mouth was always full with tobacco saliva. His dead nephew's children had never liked him, but if he was aware of that he did not let it worry him. They were only children, too young to know that one's horrible face did not necessarily mean an equally horrible mind. He was right: Nna-nndo did not like his face and did not like his mind — it did not matter to him whether the mind was full of good intentions or not, he simply could not like a face with so many deformities.

"You know that you are the heir to your father. He is not with us now, but he is standing right there where you are, watching us invisible. Do you understand?"

Nna-nndo nodded his head up and down. He did understand.

"Good," said Uncle Richard, "You see," he said with triumph to all his listeners who were now crowding round them. "You see," he went on, his voice quavering as dangerously as ever, "our brother lying down there is dead, but he is not dead. He has left a man behind him. He may be a very young man now, a little boy, but in a few years' time we shall forget the first Ezekiel Odia; we shall remember and speak of his son Nna-nndo, because he will grow to do great things." On and on he talked, getting very warm with the strength in his own words. Then the crescendo of his voice flagged and so did his energy. He moved closer to Nna-nndo, gasping for breath, his aged, bony, bare chest wheezing audibly.

"My son, which group of mourners do you wish to stay by your dead father?"

Nna-nndo looked blank.

Another man from the crowd came forward and asked loudly: "Nna-nndo, do you want your father to be in heaven with the angels, or do you want him down in the earth?"

"I want my father in Heaven!" shouted the poor boy before he could stop himself. His imagination, at the words "heaven" and "angels", had conjured up the beautiful and graceful pictures he had been shown in his lessons at the local Sunday school.

41

There was a mild murmur of anger from Uncle Richard and some of the older men. But the women seemed jubilant. They preferred Nna to go to heaven, because heaven sounded purer, cleaner and, to cap it all, the heaven of the Christians was new, and foreign; anything imported was considered to be much better than their own old ways. Chairs were quickly arranged round the open coffin and the Christians sat themselves down, singing from weighty Ibo hymn books. The young choristers clutched their hymnals in one hand and the bundles of their cassocks and surplices in the other. Uzo cleared the big bed, took the bundles from the choristers and placed these on it. The choir boys now had freedom to sing with gusto and without interference.

The time soon came for the coffin to be sealed, for Ezekiel Odia to go his own way and never be seen again in this world. Aku-nna was told to make ready a gift for her father. She was expected to give a dress, and Nna-nndo was to give a shirt. Ma Blackie's relatives searched the whole room for some article of clothing which had been worn by her, and eventually they fished out an old headtie that Ma Blackie had probably forgotten in her hurry to go home to Ibuza to have her fertility recharged.

It was necessary for the children to present their gifts, and the two of them stood there, staring at what was left of their father. *Why has he shrunk so?* Aku-nna asked herself. *What have they done to my father? I recognise that brown suit, all right — his best suit, which he had cleaned ready for the coming harvest. But the person in that suit looks so different from our father who walked out of this very room only three weeks ago telling us to be good children.* She was too frightened to look straight at the face, but out of the corner of her eye she could see that that forehead was too smooth to belong to her living father. He looked different in death. Their father had gone. The image of the father she knew would forever be in her heart. Her small-voiced father with his large bloodshot eyes containing little worm-like crisscrosses in them, her father who had a funny way of whistling when he was intoxicated with palm wine, her father whose work clothes she had to wash every Sunday, her father, who had pampered and spoiled her, who would listen to her rather than to anybody else . . . had gone. This thing they called his body was somebody else altogether. Her own father had gone.

She noticed that the Christians had stopped singing. Even her brother Nna-nndo was shocked into silence. This was death, real and in their family. The children had never seen a dead person before; that the first dead person they were to see was their father multiplied the shock. Nna-nndo was led forward to give his little gift, and Aku-nna was asked to do likewise. It was then that she summoned up the courage to look at the face. It was indeed her father's face; it was unwrinkled, smooth, almost young and the mouth was closed in such a way that he seemed about to say something to her. Then it appeared to the onlookers that she lost her senses, for instead of giving her little dress, she started to appeal to Nna to speak to her. Someone snatched the dress from her hand and flung it at the foot of the coffin.

"Leave me!" Aku-nna screamed. "He wants to tell me something. He can't just go like that. . . . He wants so say some. . . ." She lost consciousness, and did not know anything any more.

The procession to the cemetery was one of the most impressive Akinwunmi Street had ever witnessed. The railway people had brought their special hearse, with the words NIGERIAN RAILWAY DEPT written crazily in gold on the sides. Nna's body was deposited in the centre of it, flanked by his work colleagues. Nna-nndo and his sister followed, held tightly by relatives. Then came the choristers, now properly robed in their black and white outfits. Hundreds of casual friends, neighbours followed on, anybody who felt like joining the procession. The Ibuza mourners brought up the rear with their death songs and farewell dancing, the beaded gourds they carried jarring in the air. A horn-blower was present, blowing and blowing until his face was like two big, brown and shiny balloons, held together by a sweating forehead. Other men had empty bottles and tin teaspoons; they knocked the spoons against the bottles, helping to produce some kind of music.

The trouble was that there was too much music, with the horn pipe, the empty bottles, the beaded gourds, the hand-clapping, the feet-stamping, the Christians' cry for the New Jerusalem. It all became a confusion. But still the procession inched its way to the cemetery at Igbobi.

Nna's body was lowered into the grave. The gravediggers stood on each side, their tops bared and their khaki shorts all muddy. They seemed impatient. One passed a piece of dry kolanut to the other as the vicar of All Saints Church was saying, "Ashes to

43

ashes and earth to earth. . . ."

Nobody cried anymore. All tears had already been shed. Aku-nna, still weak from her earlier swoon, moved mechanically as if pulled by a string. She watched her brother pour two handfuls of sand over Nna. She did the same. Everyone seemed to be released from a trance and poured sand, stone, anything around onto Nna. It was no use begging them to be gentle, Aku-nna reasoned; Nna could not feel it.

The gravediggers, still chewing their kolanut furiously, shovelled spadeful upon spadeful on the coffin. They were so heartles, even absentminded. They simply shovelled and shovelled. The heavy clatter produced by the stones and the sand on the unprotected coffin was like a final goodbye from Ezekiel to his children.

"Always remember that you are mine," he had said only three weeks before.

Aku-nna noticed that her brother Nna-nndo was standing alone. She walked up to him, touched his hand, and together they left the cemetery.

The Ibuza people have a saying that on the day of blood relatives, friends go.

4

Return to Ibuza

Ma Blackie made her way every morning to Ezukwu, the place in Ibuza where her medicine-man lived. She had to be up very early, at the crow of the first cock. She was not to wash her face, or chew any chewing-stick, or talk to anyone, but was just to walk very fast, in the dewy mornings, to the medicine-man's hut. There she would gulp down the roots mixture which was rapidly fermenting, and tasted like a kind of wild but unsugared wine. She would wash her face with some of it, and then enter the hut to give the medicine-man his special greeting — "*Igwe*," which meant "the heavens", for this man was not only a medicine-man but was also a red-cap chief, and these chiefs were owners of the heavens. His reply to Ma Blackie was "*Amu-apa*," meaning "she who rocks her baby".

On this particular morning the old medicine-man noted that Ma Blackie was not her cheerful self, and he asked her why.

"I have heard that my husband is ill in Lagos," she explained. "I want to go and be with him and the children, but I still have three market days before I finish the good medicine you cooked for me. Can I take the remainder with me? I shall hide it from all the prying witches. I won't let them know that I have it with me."

The medicine-man furrowed his already wrinkled brow. He was skull-faced and very lean. Then he closed his eyes, and after a while began to swing his hairless head from side to side. He opened his tobacco-darkened mouth and started to make some jibbering sounds which were very unnerving. Ma shrank further away into the corner of the hut. When the man opened his eyes again they were as red as ripe palm kernels. His black mouth was producing white soap-like foam, which he wiped with the back of one of his hands then rubbed it on his loin cloth.

"Don't worry now about my medicine," he said. "If you take

it from here, those witches who are my enemies will turn it into poison. Instead of bringing you children, it may turn you into a barren woman. We shall not worry about that now. You must go and pack. Your children need you. Do not allow yourself to see today's morning sun in Ibuza. Get up, and be on your way."

There were millions of questions Ma Blackie wanted to ask him. She would have liked to know whether she could have another child for her husband when she got to Lagos, or whether she would have to return to Ibuza after her husband was better. If the medicine-man sensed all this, he was not talking. At least he was not talking the kind of language Ma Blackie could understand, for he went on jibbering, his eyes closed, his mouth foaming. His incantations assumed that peculiar whoop and call of a forest nation dancing in file.

Ma stared fearfully for just a second before she fled. She had been warned not to linger in Ibuza to see the rising sun. There was very little time.

She had been sharing a hut with Ozubu, one of the wives of her brother-in-law Okonkwo. Ma woke Ozubu and related to her in whispers what the medicine-man had just told her. Ozubu, a plump woman, was well known in the village for her simplicity, but she seemed clever all of a sudden.

"I did not wish to interfere," she said to Ma Blackie, "but I felt you should have gone back to Lagos as soon as the message came that your husband Ezekiel was ill. If I had been you, I should not have minded what Okonkwo our husband was saying." Okonkwo was Ezekiel's elder brother, and in Ibuza one's brother-in-law was also given the title of husband.

"I should have gone," Ozubu went on. "Don't worry now; if there had been anything wrong that medicine-man, that *dibia* would have told you. He is so powerful, you know, that he does not walk about in the afternoons. Rumour has it that if he sees you outside his hut in the afternoon you will just go home and sleep your last sleep, from which you will never wake up. If he says you must not see the sun rise in Ibuza today, then you are not going to see it. You will be at the motor park in Asaba by then."

"Should I not tell our husband Okonkwo first?" Ma asked, her voice dry with apprehension.

"Don't tell him yet," snarled Ozubu. Then she laughed, a low sound with no mirth in it. "He will curse you if you go near him now. Have you not noticed that for the past two market days he has been calling only Ezebona into his hut and nobody else? What makes me feel shame for them is that they stay there until the sun rises. I know that Ezebona is young and still new as his wife, but they don't seem to care what other people think. When I was new, he had not had me all that long before I was pregnant with his son. I don't know where that dry stick Ezebona is going to get children from. Maybe he will send her to the same *dibia* you go to. He would not mind spending all his money on her. But if I or my other mate," Ozubu was referring to Okonkwo's other wife, "complained of a headache, he would remind us that he paid twenty pounds on our heads.

"So don't bother to let him know until you are quite ready to go."

Ma Blackie, who was in no mood to listen to Ozubu's moanings about the husband she shared with two other women, went on packing. She hoped that Okonkwo would have stirred from his marital bed by the time she was ready to leave. She shed silent tears at the uncertainty of it all. If only that medicine-man had told her for sure what was happening to her family in Lagos, then she might at least have been able to look forward to her arrival there with some hope. As it was she could not hope, especially with people like Ozubu being so careful to tell her what she should do, that she ought to have gone back to Lagos when the news first came of Ezekiel's illness. But how was she to go, when her brother-in-law who was supposed to stand in place of her own husband refused to let her, saying that Ezekiel probably had just a slight fever and would want her to stay and be seen by the medicine-man? Where, Okonkwo asked, were there any clever medicine-men in Lagos? Why, all they had there were those people they called "dokitas" who poured poison water into you and called it medicine. Ma Blackie, he affirmed, was to stay in Ibuza and have her system purified by the clear and unpolluted water from the Oboshi river; the river and the goddess of the river were gifts to all Ibuza people from the greater gods. It was the right of all Ibuza's sons and daughters to come to have themselves cleansed by the river whenever they found themselves in difficulties in distant places of work.

Ma Blackie did not dispute all that; but why was she feeling

47

so guilty about not having returned to Lagos earlier? She consoled herself that she probably could not have done anything anyway. She chided herself for letting her imagination take hold of her. Her children were all right, her husband's foot might be playing him up again but that had been going on for over five years now, since he came back from the army. Why should it suddenly become serious just when she was not with him?

There was one thing she was determined to do: for once she was going to disobey Okonkwo. She knew that a woman should always obey an elderly brother-in-law, but now she could not care less. She would do exactly what Ozubu had suggested, though for different reasons. Ozubu would regard it as a slight on Okonkwo, but Ma Blackie was worrying about her family.

Luck was with her. Just as she was coming out of the *owele*, the women's lavatory, she saw Okonkwo's youngest wife Ezebona rushing in. He must have finished with her then. Ma walked very fast, her feet crumbling the dried leaves as she went. When she reached the egbo tree which marked the boundary of Okonkwo's personal compound, she called out her morning greeting to him.

He answered her with her special greeting, "*Amu-apa!*" and came out wearing his farm loin cloth. One look at her face told him that all was not well, and he invited her inside.

They sat on the raised mud pavement which ran round the whole hut and served as sitting places. The biggest room at the front served as a sitting apartment, and it had a roof window which caved in to let in light and also to allow for a good collection of rain water. The centre apartment slept both the humans as well as the animals — goats and rams — of the family. At the extreme end of this open and partially roofless space were some goatskins and wooden headrests which had not yet been tidied away. Ozubu was right, thought Ma Blackie; Okonkwo slept with his new wife till the second crow of the cock!

Ma did not let that bother her; neither was she troubled by the smell of the goats' droppings and urine which still hung heavily in the air. She simply told her brother-in-law what the medicine-man had said.

Okonkwo raised himself, lifted his loin cloth and folded it inwards into a sort of triangular envelope at the front, inside which he rested his genitals, leaving his whole back side bare. Then he sat down again on the cool mud bench, blowing away from his face the flies which the goats' excretions had invited. He was thinking; and, judging from the ugly way his face looked, his thoughts were not happy ones.

"You must go," he said at last. "And if Ezekiel blames you for going back without finishing your treatment, tell him I said you were to do so. Remind him, in case he has forgotten, that I am the eldest and first son of our father. It is for me to say the word, and for Ezekiel to obey. Tell him that. Off with you."

Ezebona came in then to sweep out the courtyard-like apartment with a long hand-broom made of weeds tied together. Her husband watched her young and lithe body, his eyes drawn to the bluish bridal tattoo that worked outwards from the middle of Ezebona's bare breasts and met at the centre of her back. He caught Ma following his eyes and immediately checked his gaze and collected himself.

"Leave that now," he told Ezebona. "Blackie is going back to her husband and children today. She will need one of you to help her carry her box to Asaba. You must come straight back; I don't want to hear that you are at Cable Point in Asaba gossiping with women who have nothing to do. So as soon as the mammy-lorry has left with Ma, you must come home at once. I want to see you when I return from the farm."

"I have heard you," replied Ezebona, and turned to look inquiringly at Ma Blackie. "I hope all is well, with you rushing away and leaving us like this?"

Ma did not know what suddenly took hold of her. Maybe it was jealousy. Okonkwo was wiry and tall, with a haughty stoop, and had been a handsome man in his youth (so handsome that his first wife had run to him without his having to pay a penny for her bride price). Her husband Ezekiel was younger, shorter, and slightly pot-bellied as a result of the comparatively easier life he had led in Lagos. That Okonkwo cared more for this Ezebona than Ezekiel did for Ma was apparent. That Ezebona should be glorying in it was too much. Ma Blackie felt she just could not take any more that morning.

"If all was well," she snapped at the innocent girl, "would I be rushing away like this, like a mad woman? Were you not brought up by a mother at all? You have not given me a morning greeting — you saw me at the *owele* and did not say a word to me — and now just because our husband is here you ask me if all is well.

Do you really care whether all is well or not?" She marched out, crumbling the egbo leaves on the ground under her bare feet.

Ezebona gazed at her husband in wordless appeal. What had she done now? For a while Okonkwo said nothing, then he spoke in a low, smooth voice:

"Fill my tobacco pipe for me. Come and sit here, while you do it."

Ezebona sat beside him, and he began to trace with his forefingers along the lines made by the blue bridal tattoo. He asked her if she had cried a lot the day the tattoo woman cut the little lines.

Ezebona smiled. She went back to their sleeping area, where the goatskins were still lying and the fire was still glowing. She made an attempt to pick up a live charcoal to put in the clay pipe, but it burned her fingers. Okonkwo came forward, telling her in that smooth yet urgent voice that he had warned her several times not to touch live fire with her bare fingers. She would get burned. He demanded to see the hurt finger, then spat on it, gently rubbing in the moisture with one hand while the other hand continued tracing and retracing the blue tattoo marks on his young wife's bare body. He sat down on the goatskins on the floor, one leg stretched out, the other bent, and Ezebona placed her plaited head on his arched thigh. They remained like that for some time, Okonkwo puffing peacefully at his tobacco and telling her intimate little nothings. Then he took a long draw on his pipe and sighed deeply.

Ezebona's head shot up. "All is well?" she asked again.

Okonkwo shook his head. "My brother . . . my brother. . . ."

"Is he very ill? Has there been another sad message?"

He looked at her, long and sadly. "You are a pretty woman, like a goddess. And a goddess who does not open her mouth too much will always be mysterious and beautiful. Hurry now, and help that woman take her things to Asaba. Remember to keep your mouth shut, and don't annoy her further. She is very upset. Run."

Ma Blackie had begged the driver to drop her in front of a house in Wakeham Street where one of her cousins, Maggie, lived with her husband Ageh. It was still very early when they arrived and

50

there were few people about. Ma thanked the driver for his kindness, and called loudly for her cousin from the front of the house. They must have been asleep, for Ma had to call several times before there was a faint answer from inside. Maggie must have recognised her voice.

"Is it you, Blackie? Oh, dear . . . *e-wo*. . . ."

Ma Blackie's heart sank. Why did Maggie sound so pathetic? She heard hurried movements and murmurings from the house. Lights were going on in different rooms, for most of the occupants knew Ma Blackie well. They began to rush out of the house. One look at Ma told them that she had not heard what had happened, otherwise she would surely have arrived here in Lagos in mourning. It was obvious that she was worried, and she had the untidy appearance of someone who had had to travel in great haste, but she was wearing ordinary clothes.

Ma peered hard to see the faces of her cousin and friends, who were all trying to look away. Maggie lifted Ma's wooden box onto her head, another woman, Oyibo's mother, carried Ma's big basket which contained a few yams and heads of plantain. Ma Blackie had been in too much of a hurry to bring anything for her children.

She asked them how her husband Ezekiel was, and she was told that he had arrived from hospital only the day before. Ma Blackie danced for joy in the street at that early hour. Relief worked its way through her tensed body, releasing her tongue. She chatted to her listeners, describing the anxiety she had been through, telling them how worried she had been, how she was so happy to be back. She did note to herself that everyone was unusually quiet, and seemed to be allowing her to rattle on; but she was frightened to ask why it was. Intuition told her that something had gone wrong with her family, but like most humans she would rather delay the hearing of it until it became inevitable.

They were making their way to the house in Akinwunmi Street where Ma Blackie had lived with her husband and children before returning to Ibuza, and as they turned from Queen's Street into Akinwunmi Street she felt her heart beating very fast. Doubts mixed with fear lumped in her chest, and the lump seemed to be rising to her throat, about to choke her. She stopped talking. They rounded the little corner adjacent to the public house known as The Club, and then were facing the house.

51

Ma began to move forward in a trot, like someone possessed, then turned the trot into a run. What had happened? Why were there so many chairs? Why was the ground so trodden? Where were her children? Her silent questioning confronted her cousin Maggie, who found herself telling one more lie, unconvincing even to herself:

"Ezekiel celebrated his discharge from hospital and they have not yet returned the chairs. . . ."

"Really?" Ma Blackie asked doubtfully.

She was not given much time to ponder on this, because Maggie started to shout, calling their Ibo neighbours. Then Ma Blackie was being ushered into the room. There was no need now for anyone to tell her what had happened.

Busy hands unthreaded her hair. She was stripped of her clothes and given an older, torn set to put on. A place on the cemented floor was cleared for her to sit and cry and mourn for her dead husband.

Weeks later, Ma Blackie and her two children were ready to set out for their home town, Ibuza. This was the only thing to be done, when the head of a family was no more. Life in Lagos, like life in all capital cities, cost a great deal of money, and was not possible without a breadwinner. In the Odia family, the breadwinner had gone, so his dependants had to go back home to fend for themselves as best they could. There was nothing else to do; they had to go.

It was a bright and clear morning when the sad little group left Akinwunmi Street. Neighbours wished them goodbye with small gifts and with tears. The children were sorry indeed to leave the only life they had known, their friends, their Lagos relatives — especially Uncle Joseph and Uncle Uche who had looked after them since their sick father had gone into hospital. But they were told they must leave it all behind, and face a new life in Ibuza.

Aku-nna remembered only scraps of stories about what life in Ibuza would be like. She knew she would have to marry, and that the bride price she would fetch would help to pay the school fees for her brother Nna-nndo. She did not mind that; at least it would mean that she would be well fed. What she feared was the type of man who would be chosen for her. She would have liked to marry someone living in Lagos, so that she would not have to work on a farm and carry cassava. She had heard stories of how strenuous farm life could be for a woman. She had heard that a farmer husband did not give housekeeping money, as her father had given her mother. There were so many questions she would have liked to ask, but it was regarded as bad manners to be too inquisitive. So Aku-nna listened, worried and prayed to God to help them all.

This morning, when they were leaving Lagos for good, Uncle Uche sent for a "truck-man". All their belongings had been gathered together and had to be packed onto a hand-cart and taken to the place where they were to board the lorry for Ibuza. The truck-man turned out to be Ibo; the Ibo people have a reputation for not minding what job they take on, so long as it brings money — a race who are particularly business-mad. He was short, very black, not at all handsome, but young and very charming, and he said that for five shillings he would pull the Odias' possessions to Iddo motor park.

"Five shillings!" protested Ma Blackie. "Do you think I am going home for a holiday or for Christmas? Can't you see my clothes? Don't you know that the husband who brought me to this town as a young girl-bride is no more? What part of Iboland did you come from? If I had called an Ngbati truck-man, a Yoruba man, I am sure he would pity my condition and charge me less. But oh, no, not us Ibos! All we know is money, money, money! We value money so much that we forget the fear of God."

Ma Blackie's voice started to wobble. Tears were already pouring from her eyes along the clan tattooes on her cheeks. She sniffed then undid one side of her black mourning lappa and blew her nose into it.

The truck-man looked this way and that like a trapped animal seeking an escape route. He must have been blind, he admitted. He had not looked closely. Of course he was a proper Ibo man, he said, drawing his little body up and pulling his mud-soaked shorts towards his naked belly at the same time. He would take less money. He would take only four shillings. If the truck had been his own, he would have taken them free.

"But, you see," he went on, lifting his eyes to the heavens where God is supposed to live, "I have to live and feed my family too. I do not pray for my wife to go home like this, but when death strikes we humans are helpless."

"You have spoken well, my friend," contributed Uncle Uche. "Take my dead brother's things to Iddo motor park. God would not let your family go home this way. But take three shillings."

"Yes, three shillings, three shillings," sang the voices of Maggie, Uzo and many of the women standing by. "Please take three shillings, and God bless you."

The truck-man hitched up his khaki shorts once more. Then he heaved the sigh of someone forced into a decision.

"All right, three shillings and sixpence, and let us go. If you are not there early you miss the good lorries." He began to heave the truck round ready to roll it down to the motor park.

The women nodded their heads and made conspiratorial signs to Ma Blackie assuring her that she had made a good bargain. The truck-man pretended not to see the nods but in fact missed nothing. He rolled the truck into the middle of the road, crunching the pebbles under its wheels. He was all set to go.

There were final farewells, and the party left Akinwunmi Street. At Oyingbo Market they met many of their town's women on their way to sell dried fish; they all put down their fish baskets, everyone cried a little, and the family were given some sea fish. Comfort's mother gave Aku-nna a threepenny piece and Nna-nndo two new pennies. They wished Ma Blackie luck, and continued, subdued, into the market.

There was not much argument about price at the motor park, for it turned out that the church to which they belonged had taken care of the necessary arrangements. This so surprised Ma Blackie that she began to weep again.

"People have been so kind," she cried into her mourning cloth.

Mama Emeka and Mrs Gibson, the two representatives of the Ibo section of All Saints Church, had already told the sad story of Ma's predicament to the driver of a mammy-wagon, and the driver was so sorry that he reserved a special back seat for the family. There they would be able to sit and rest against the bundles of stock-fish that were being transported to the Eastern Region of Nigeria. Their position at the back would also ensure that they had a supply of fresh air, for these seats were near the side openings of the lorry.

"I prefer to sit and lean against bundles of stock-fish," observed Emeka's mother. "At least dead fish don't talk, and they don't push and grumble if you rest your head against them in the middle of the night."

Ma Blackie and Mrs Gibson agreed with her, and the former added:

"We have been very fortunate. I wonder who the man is that agreed to be so kind without even knowing us."

"Oh, there he is. You see that man running, with a beard and wearing a checked shirt? That's him."

Meanwhile the man with the beard was busy negotiating and urging customers to board his lorry. A family who seemed well-to-do was approaching the motor park: a young man who was well dressed and had the look and carriage of a civil servant, his pretty wife and very little son. The drivers from all ten waiting lorries ran like birds let loose from an aviary towards the young family, but the bearded driver shot past them all, snatched the biggest suitcase from the protesting group and ran to the front of his lorry. He smiled with triumph when the young husband had to come after him with the cry:

"Eh, look, I have valuables in that box! Careful you don't break them."

The driver, pampering the suitcase like a new-born baby, gave his assurance that the things would be well taken care of. "You wouldn't get the same treatment in other lorries, I can tell you that. Myself and my mate — you see him over there, that man chewing kolanuts — well, we are the best drivers this Iddo motor park has ever seen. Our lorry is the biggest, and there are the two of us to drive it, so when I am tired he takes over from me. We also have a mechanic on board. This is a special lorry, for the likes of you — big men who know what quality means and who like to travel in comfort."

He paused, arched his brow to his mate the second driver who walked briskly to collect the family's other luggage from the other less aggressive drivers. There were murmurs and grumbled protests from his competitors, but the bearded driver ignored them. He and the well-dressed family man began to discuss the fare in lowered voices. At one stage of the negotiations, the well-dressed man made as if dissatisfied and seemed about to make a move towards the other lorries, but Emeka's mother, who had been watching the goings-on, shouted,

"Go in his lorry! He is the best of them all. And moreover, you will be sure of arriving at Asaba in good time."

The bearded driver gave Emeka's mother a grateful smile. He spread his hands in a gesture that seemed to say, "You see what I mean?" To the watching women the argument appeared over; the civil servant seemed satisfied with the arrangement, for the assistant driver was now stacking his belongings into the "mammy-lorry".

Many more passengers arrived, and time and again the same process had to be gone through to hook each one of them. As she waited Ma Blackie was able to forget for a short while that Nna had died. She talked with the women about old times, about the latest designs in lappa cloths. Emeka's mother, a very well fed woman with folds of flesh circling her shiny black neck like beads, announced in her big voice that she had bought the newest material known as "Abada Lekord", which featured a design of gramophone records. Ma agreed that it was a very attractive design and that the colour looked as if it would stay fast.

"You can wash and wash material like that and the colour remains bright as though it is still new." She sighed, maybe remembering that she would never be able to afford any now that her husband had gone.

The others got the message and sighed too. Emeka's mother looked round the now very busy motor park, and felt almost ashamed at her enthusiasm. She noticed Aku-nna standing alone, her back against the lorry that was soon to take them home.

"I think your daughter is hungry," she said turning to Ma. "I must see if I can get the children something to eat. Do you want anything, Blackie?"

Ma Blackie shook her head.

"I should eat something if I were you," intervened Mrs Gibson. "The journey is long and you may not find the type of food you like at Abeokuta and Benin."

"I know," replied Ma. "But the point is that I am always sick on this journey, and if my stomach is empty I will not feel so bad."

"I see," concluded Emeka's mother. "Aku-nna . . . aaa . . .!" she called, raising her voice louder than ever as if she was calling the whole motor park to attention. "Nna-nndo . . . oooo! Come, both of you, and let me buy you some food."

Many heads turned to the direction of the call. The driver with the beard strolled towards them, breathing like a man who had done good business and was quite pleased with the result. He flashed his white teeth and said to the group, "Don't worry about the money."

He plunged his hand into the big leather shoulder-bag he was carrying and gave Aku-nna five shillings. "Go to the food counter at the railway station across the road and buy something for yourself and your brother. The food there is cleaner than what you get at the open stalls. Hurry up now. I've got enough passengers so I shall be moving soon."

The women stared at him with round eyes. All of five shillings for a little girl to spend on food! Ma Blackie was so touched that she had to wipe her eyes with the edge of her mourning lappa. Emeka's mother sang loud the praises of the man with the beard, and Mrs Gibson and Auntie Uzo thanked him profusely. When Uzo went on to point out that such men usually ended up rich because God blessed their kindness, all the women nodded their agreement to this philosophy. He would one day surely be a rich man.

Soon afterwards it was time for all Ma Blackie's friends and neighbours to leave to go home, in time to welcome their husbands back from work at four o'clock. They were sorry for Ma Blackie and her family and had given all the help they could, but the time had come to see to their own lives as well, their own children and husbands. It had to be goodbye. The parting was elongated with speeches, pieces of advice to Aku-nna in particular, and prayers for Ma. More tears were shed, and then the friends all left.

The intense and suffocating heat of the afternoon had given way to a caressingly mild warmth. Shadows were long; a gentle wind blew from the lagoon. The sun was preparing to make its disappearance and had moved downwards from the centre of the sky to a side of it. Tired salesmen and drivers sat in the shade drinking chilled palm wine. Food-sellers were eating their leftovers. The lorry drivers strolled lazily round their vehicles, checking this and checking that, not too keen to start the long journey.

Aku-nna and Nna-nndo stared at the final preparations taking place. They still could not really believe that they were actually leaving Lagos at last. Lagos where all their childhood had been spent. Lagos where all their friends lived. Lagos where the body of their father lay in an unmarked grave somewhere at Igbobi.

Nna-nndo's lips were dry; he licked them. There was confusion in his young heart. Yet it could not be helped. He had to go.

All the passengers had mounted now. The mammy-lorry groaned, shook from side to side like a huge earthquake, eased itself from its resting place, coughed out loud smoke, started to move jerkily . . . then suddenly gathered speed. Among the waving hands of the few friends and relatives who remained to see the passengers off were those of Auntie Uzo and Uncle Uche. Voices cried, "Safe journey!"

The sheds and food-stalls started to move by fast, and soon they were in the main road. A sweat-soaked traffic warden with bold zebra-like tribal markings on his shiny face waved them on. The mammy-lorry raced forwards at a lunatic speed, out of Lagos.

5

Life in Ibuza

The mammy-lorry sped through Shagamu and Okitipupa and many
other Yoruba towns. At first the children were fascinated by the
speed of the passing houses which, they noticed, were mainly built
of mud and had walls that were not as smooth as those of the
houses they were used to seeing in Lagos. Thick forests seemed
forever about to swallow them up, but somehow the road always
managed to continue despite this tropical jungle. There were cocoa
and kolanut trees along the roads bordering several towns, and the
pods carrying the kolanuts hung downwards like a pregnant
woman's breasts.

After Shagamu, the traders in the lorry burst into song. Travelling to and from Lagos was their way of life. They would buy cloth,
stock-fish and cartons of imported foodstuffs in Lagos, and most
of the traders would take these buys to Asaba and across the River
Niger to the big market in Onitsha where they could sell their
ware. The more ambitious of the traders would travel further
inland to places like Aba and thereby make more profit. The money
they received from selling there was used to buy yams, bags of
garri and other produce from the local farmers which was then
taken back for sale in Lagos. The Ibo traders along this route
were well known for their fast developing little empires. They
patronised the many roadside food stalls which provided pounded
yam and soup with chunky pieces of bush-meat. There were also
kegs and kegs of palm wine to wash it all down.

In the lorry carrying Ma Blackie and her children, three-quarters
of the passengers were such traders. They were in the habit of
making their travelling enjoyable by making up songs for the
driver, songs about anything they might see along the way. Young
girls on their way to the streams were the most popular topic, and
as they passed yet another stream and yet another group of girls

the songs became more and more funny. Aku-nna wondered why girls along this road never bothered to cover the tops of their bodies, and mostly wore nothing except some coloured loin cloth. Of course the traders composed lyrics about girls with mosquito legs, girls with breasts like pumpkins, girls with hair on their chests.

Palm wine from different towns was another subject for song composition. Ubulu-okoti, for instance, was an Ibo town reputed for its tasty and intoxicating brew. Everyone — traders, women, children and even the élite passengers — joined in nostalgic songs about this town, her wine and her young girls with breasts as big as calabashes. The climax came when the driver, too, took up the refrain in his own special baritone voice, and even began to drive the lorry in tune with the music: as the pitch of the song rose, so he would change to a higher gear, creating the impression that the mammy-lorry itself was rocking to the music. It was indeed a melodious drive to Asaba.

The landscape changed slightly after Benin. The soil was redder, the leaves were that type of deep green which suggests a tinge of black. The forests became really dense like mysterious groves. Here you saw a narrow footpath like a red ribbon winding itself into the mysterious depths. There you saw a human figure emerge as it were from a secret green retreat, carrying on her head a bunch of ripe, blood-coloured palm fruits. Or a girl with her little sister, scrambling into the deep forest at the sound of the approaching lorry.

Near a town called Agbor, they passed a stream which Ma Blackie told her inquisitive children was known as "Ologodo". Aku-nna nodded; her godmother was said to be from Agbor Ologodo. Aku-nna wondered to herself: so this was the place the woman came from. It was difficult to associate this little stream beside which girls and women bathed with her godmother who had become so rich and fashionable in Lagos. These people too, like those near the Yoruba towns, dressed scantily, and those of them who were well dressed, presumably on their way to the markets, wore their headscarves tied at what seemed to Aku-nna funny angles. They were out of touch with Lagos fashions, Ma Blackie explained.

There was something else different about the people here; they seemed more relaxed, more naturally beautiful than their relatives in Lagos. The women all had such long necks and carried their heads high, like ostriches, as if they had a special pride in themselves, and their gracefully thin legs lent their whole appearance extra height. It was only the old people who could be seen to stoop. Every other person moved with such bearing that gave them a natural, untutored elegance.

Then the lorry passed a market — compared with the big ones in Lagos it was a toy market, but it was certainly noisier. The smell of fresh cassava mingled with that of live fish and palm oil, and in the heat and humidity the smell seemed to hang in the air, heavy and tangible.

Very early the next morning they arrived in Asaba. As Emeka's mother had predicted the day before, theirs was the first lorry to arrive from Iddo motor park. Their driver had indeed been very fast; he had probably been spurred on by the flattering songs of his passengers. Aku-nna, who had grown rapidly in mind since her father's death, noted that despite the early hour all the male traders disappeared into the town. Ma explained to her that most rich traders kept mistresses there, and when they arrived so early they went to the houses of their girlfriends to spend the rest of the night. This revelation shocked Aku-nna a little, especially since their bearded driver was one of the first to take his leave, carrying a bush paraffin lamp. Did all men behave like that? Was her father like that? Was the well-dressed civil-servant, who still clung to his sleeping wife, like that? No, Aku-nna told herself. Her father had been different, and so was this civil-servant. That the clerk behind his wife's back might behave in the same way as the traders did not occur to Aku-nna.

The whole adult world was becoming too complicated, so Aku-nna stopped thinking about it, followed her mother's example and dropped off to sleep. With most of the traders gone to their Asaba sweethearts, there was now more room for tired bodies to stretch out.

They were awakened by a rice-seller hawking very near the motor park.

"You'll come again if you taste this one. . . . Just come and taste it! You will lick your fingers. . . . I have plenty of onions in it . . . plenty of whiteman's pepper in it. . . . I have ripe tomatoes in it. . . . If you taste this one, you will come again. . . ."
The seller went on singing the praises of her cooked rice.

Aku-nna peeped through the tarpaulin that covered the lorry and saw the rice — yellow with some green leafy vegetables working criss-cross among the grains. The rice must be hot, for even from a distance she could see the thick steam puffing out of the giant pot. Despite herself, her mouth watered at the sight.

Nna-nndo woke up their mother, and insisted that he was hungry and would have nothing in this world but that particular rice. Ma Blackie remonstrated mildly.

"But you have not washed your face, son. Look, my daughter, take your brother to the bank of the river. You must both have a wash. Our people will be here at sunrise, because today is Nkwo market day. I don't want them to see you both looking dirty and covered in mud. Take this calabash and bring me some water so that I may wash my face too."

"But I want to buy some rice from the rice-seller, before she finishes selling it all," Nna-nndo complained to Ma.

"Well, you must wash your face and clean your teeth before eating any rice."

"My teeth are clean, and I had a bath yesterday."

"No wash, no rice, you hear me? Don't you have any pity on your poor mother? Listen, your father is dead. I am the only person left to look after you. You will kill me before my time if you keep arguing with me like that and not doing what you are told at once. Go, wash your face, you bush man."

"Yes, he is a bush man." The civil-servant, who had been listening to the altercation between mother and son, intervened, laughing. "Bush men don't wash their faces. Did you not eat yesterday? Well, then, before you eat today you must wash."

Nna-nndo felt ashamed of himself. He followed his sister meekly, glancing furtively once or twice in the direction of the steaming rice but finally resigning himself to doing as he was told. He did not at all like being called a bush man.

The sun soon rose, warm and golden. The children had been fed on the hot rice, and Ma Blackie and many of the other passengers had had the corn custard known as *ogi* and akara balls. They were all washed, and their luggage was stacked neatly on the damp grass by the roadside. The regular traders who had before light gone into town were now coming back, one by one. Their eyes looked tired. And though they did not look like men who had passed a peaceful night they seemed contented enough, some puffing thoughtfully on clay pipes like goats chewing grass.

"Our people will be here soon," Ma Blackie said. "They will take our things for us, so we won't have a lot to carry."

"Is it very far to Ibuza, Mother?" Aku-nna asked.

"No, not far, only seven miles. We shall be home before all the farmers have gone to the farm. Ah, look! Here comes the first group of our people. They've seen us!"

The children stared in the direction their mother was pointing and saw about fifteen women trotting into the fast filling square that was to be the market place. They were carrying a heavy pile of damp cassava pulp, all tied with banana skins onto baskets; many of the baskets were not very big, but with the heaps of dripping cassava pulp piled high on them they ended up looking like sky-scrapers. *Akpu*, as the cassava pulp was called locally, was a very heavy foodstuff made from the roots of the cassava plant — so heavy was it that the necks of the poor women carriers (who were sweating profusely although the heat of the early sun was still moderate) were compressed to half their normal sizes.

Ma Blackie called out to them, and as they came to welcome the Odia family from Lagos their sympathy was apparent. They were all sorry for Ma, and many of them assured her that they had shed all the tears their eyes were capable of shedding when the news came of the death of her husband. They would first sell their akpu in bulk, they said, then come and help Ma Blackie carry her belongings to Ibuza. Ma protested, knowing that they would make less profit by selling their akpu in bulk, but the women reminded her that, in Ibuza, the day you cried for the death of another, you cried for yourself. What were a few pennies when one of their friends was wearing black clothes? No, Ma was not to worry; they would sell in bulk to those who were remaining in Asaba for the rest of the day, then come to help her.

True to their word, in less than an hour the happy group were chattering like monkeys as the Odias were escorted back to Ibuza. Every suitcase and box found a carrier. Even Aku-nna's school books were balanced elegantly on Ogugua's head. Ogugua was Aku-nna's first cousin, one of the daughters of her father's elder brother Okonkwo. They were going to be friends, Ogugua assured her; they both belonged to the same big house, and they were also the same age.

"You know," Ogugua elaborated, "the very week you were born

63

in Lagos, I was born here in Ibuza. My parents have been telling me so much about you — that you're very clever at school and all that. Now we're going to be friends. We shall be like sisters, especially if your mother chooses to be with my father."

"Why should my mother choose your father? How come?" Aku-nna asked, puzzled. The two girls had lagged behind, engrossed in their gossip.

Ogugua burst out laughing. "You're almost fourteen years old now and you still don't know the customs of our Ibuza people? Your mother is inherited by my father, you see, just as he will inherit everything your father worked for."

"Oh, dear!" exclaimed Aku-nna, as if in physical pain. "How can my mother fit into that type of life?"

"So, why should you worry about that? Look, you see that woman in front? Can you see her?" Ogugua was pointing to one of the women accompanying them on the walk home. The woman was very thin and walked with a limp on skinny legs. She seemed happy enough, chatting away with Ma Blackie and the others. On her head she balanced a basket containing Ma's cooking pots, wooden spoons and few metal plates, and as she talked she gesticulated with long, bony arms. No doubt she had been glad to get rid of her akpu in order to help Ma carry home some of her sophisticated utensils from Lagos.

"What about her?" Aku-nna asked, eyeing her cousin with suspicion.

"Her husband was a big man in a white man's job, somewhere in the Hausa hills. Well, three years ago he died suddenly. A lorry knocked him down. He was ground to such a pulp that you couldn't recognise him. You know why he died like that?"

Aku-nna shook her head. She did not know.

Ogugua pulled her further back, so that the older women would not overhear what she was about to tell Aku-nna. The latter saw something of her father in Ogugua's eyes, which like her own were large and expressive. But that was not where the family likeness ended: the squarish face not yet rounded out with fatty flesh, the swing of the arms, which gave the impression that they were boneless, were also part of the family uniqueness. Ogugua was much darker, however; her skin shone now, polished by a light morning perspiration. Her legs were thicker, her voice was louder. She was bolder, too, Aku-nna noticed.

Ogugua drew her cousin nearer and whispered:

"He was sleeping with an Onitsha housewife. So the husband of the Onitsha woman put a curse on him. He didn't see where he was going, and the lorry ran him over and mashed him into a meaty pulp. Even his own child didn't recognise him!"

This was followed by a short silence, during which Aku-nna tried to imagine the meaty pulp. She spat into the bush.

"How terrible!" she gasped.

"Yes," her cousin agreed. "It was a horrible death. You see, that woman in front was his wife. He married her in church. They only had one spoilt daughter, after about ten or —" here she began to count on her fingers to check that she had calculated the figure right — "eleven years of marriage."

"How terrible! A very bad mariage indeed," observed Aku-nna.

"But listen," Ogugua went on, warming up with enthusiasm. "That woman was inherited by her husband's brother. He has a title — he's an Obi. She is not the chief wife, but she's very happy. She has everything she wants now, even a son."

Aku-nna clapped her hands with excitement at this piece of news. "It's just like the stories you read in books."

Her cousin did not know about stories in books, but she did know a great number of folk stories that were told by moonlight and handed down from generation to generation. And that was not all. Her mother had told her that the woman, Ma Beaty, had again missed two full moons of her period.

Aku-nna wanted to ask how Ogugua's mother knew but decided to keep quiet, so that her cousin would not think she did not know what menstruation was all about. She had heard talk of it and had read a book or two on the subject, but Aku-nna had not yet started having hers, so she was not quite sure of the implications of what her cousin said. However, she asked:

"You mean she is pregnant again?"

"Might be."

The gap between them and the older women had by now elongated; they could still see them but could no longer hear their voices. Suddenly Ma Blackie looked round and beckoned them with a scolding hand. She shouted at them to keep up, asking what it was that they were carrying that was holding them back so.

Aku-nna began to see her mother in a new light. A tall, straight-backed woman, with very black and gleaming skin that had earned her the admiring name "Blackie the Black Woman". Even when she talked in the dark, her teeth flashed. She was slim, but not skinny. Like her friends, she too had a powerful voice; but unlike most of them her life had been comparatively soft. Ma Blackie had never had to carry an akpu basket. Would she have to do that now, since Nna had died? Poor Mother, Aku-nna thought. She would have to work hard at school so that she could be a teacher — that's how she could help her mother. Aku-nna remembered how her father had talked of her having a higher education, but that dream had been buried with him at Igbobi. She could only pray that her uncle — her new father as he would soon be — would allow her to complete her Standard Six. Tears filled in her eyes, and she quickly wiped them away before she and Ogugua met up with the waiting adults.

The women started talking again, but the two girls were quiet. Ogugua's ears were pricked, absorbing every detail of the conversation. But Aku-nna and her young brother were lost in confused thoughts of many different things.

A bicycle bell jingled in the distance behind them. In fact there were two riders, but the bicycle of one was old and its bell did not work, despite the rider's desperate efforts. This was obviously a let-down for him, especially as the rider with the ringing bell had successfully attracted the attention of the group of women in front of them. The rider of the old bicycle tried to make up for it by riding ostentatiously in a zig-zag fashion, making the women shudder and run to the edge of the forest, leaving the road clear for the cyclists to pass.

However the riders decided not to go by, but to stop for a chat. The man on the new bicycle was a teacher at the school of the Church Missionary Society — the very church that the Odia family would be attending. He knew Ma Blackie and had heard of her husband's death, so he dismounted and greeted the women, reserving a special welcome for the bereaved family.

"The children have certainly grown. Thank God for that," he finished by way of consolation.

The women nodded, understanding what he meant. The children would soon be able to fend for themselves.

Aku-nna looked at the man. He had called them children, but he was not so old himself. Maybe eighteen or nineteen. So why call them children? He must be a very proud person. She did not listen to her mother saying that she would be doing her last year at school under the teacher. They all referred to him as The Teacher, as if that was his name, or a title or something; one would think he had no other proper name.

"Aku-nna, are you sleeping?" Ma prompted. "This is your new teacher. You will be under him." She pushed her daughter forward as if to say, *There you are, she is your pupil — teach her!*

Aku-nna smiled shyly and said, "Good morning, sir," wondering to herself why it was that some teachers were so young and others so old.

The teacher made a slight bow in acknowledgement of her greeting. He was so tall and angular that but for his colour one might have thought him foreign. His forehead was very high, like that of a man who would go bald in a few years' time, but at this moment his hair had been allowed to grow into long, tight woolly curls at the front, trimmed shorter at the sides and back in the style known as "Sugar Baby". This thick frontal hairstyle suited the teacher's narrow type of face, giving it a more rectangular shape. His chin was pointed, and he appeared to have been making some useless attempts to grow a funny kind of beard. He smiled now, displaying an even set of teeth, and then began to speak in a low, rich, slow voice, completely controlled as if it could not be susceptible to excitement. Perhaps he was not as young as he looked, thought Aku-nna.

"Would you like me to give the boy a lift home?" offered the other rider eventually. He had stood apart, watching aloof the greetings and introductions.

"Thank you, that would be a help," Ma Blackie accepted gratefully. "Hop on the bike, son, and the teacher's friend will take you home. By the way," she asked the young man, "who are your parents, and what part of Ibuza are you from?"

"My name is Okine. I am from Umuodafe, the first son of Odogwu."

"Oh, my God, my good God!" was Ma Blackie's shouted exclamation. "How come I did not recognise you? You have grown as tall as a palm tree. Aku-nna, Nna-nndo — come along and say hello to your cousin, the son of Odogwu."

Again the children were pushed forward. Aku-nna did not know whether she was expected to say, "Good morning, sir," in English as she had to the teacher, or whether she had to address him with the special greeting, *"Odozi ani"*. Confused, she and her brother simply moved forward like marionettes propelled by a great force, smiling and mumbling some form of salutation heard and understood only by themselves. It was Nna-nndo who first found his tongue and spoke up.

"Mother, we have so many cousins and uncles in Ibuza."

The others laughed, for he was right. Nearly everyone in Ibuza was related. They all knew each other, the tales of one another's ancestors, their histories and heroic deeds. Nothing was hidden in Ibuza. It was the duty of every member of the town to find out and know his neighbour's business.

For a while they all stood and chatted. The young men had that distinctive and good-humoured quality of ease which was the heritage of people who had long ago learned and absorbed the art of communal living. It was agreed that Nna-nndo, the son of the house, should accept the bicycle lift from Okine, since he was his cousin. The teacher, without doubt the wealthier of the two men, was not a close relative though he would soon be connected with the family when the children attended his school, so after some hesitation he suggested that he might give Aku-nna a lift home. There was an immediate lull within the noisy group. The songs of bush parrots could be heard, as well as the sounds made by fast moving reptiles in the bush, going their different ways on the carpet of dried leaves.

Aku-nna looked from one person to another. Were they waiting for her to decide? The bicycle was new enough. The teacher was nice and handsome. But she was surer of her own two feet than of riding on a bicycle. What if they fell? She might kill herself; it would be just like the course of the gods for there to be two deaths so close together in the same family. No, she was not going to accept. She was too nervous.

"No, thank you very much," she said aloud shortly.

Ma Blackie began to talk very rapidly and very loudly, as if all her listeners had suddenly gone deaf. "She is a coward, this daughter of mine. I knew she was going to say something like that. All her age group in Lagos knew how to ride bicycles, but not my daughter. Too frightened!"

"I don't blame her," Ma Beaty put in. "I feel afraid for the young people when they ride so fast, especially with the hills on this road. Don't worry, teacher, let her walk home with us. She is not used to all this walking, and it is high time she started to learn. She has been lagging behind all the time."

They all laughed, except Aku-nna. She tried to hide her face by looking into the bush. Yes, she was tired. She had not realised that seven miles was such a long journey on foot. But she wished the teacher and his friend would go away and stop staring at her so.

The young men were staring at her, but they did not see a coward who would not dare do what other girls of her age could do. They saw a young, pretty girl of fourteen with golden-brown skin, whose small, pointed breasts were asserting their presence under the thin nylon blouse she wore. There was a kind of delicacy about her, for she had not yet been toughened by life, as had the girls born and bred in Ibuza. Her large eyes were like cool but troubled pools in her head, and now she lifted the lids of those eyes and looked straight at the teacher, as if begging him to leave. The teacher, who despite his younger appearance was twenty-four, correctly interpreted Aku-nna's message and tapped his friend on the shoulder.

"Let us go. I am sure they would like to bathe at the Atakpo stream." He moved away a little, and then murmured, "So long, Aku."

It was a minor incident to Ma Blackie's mind, and the women soon forgot the young men and resumed their chattering as before, remarking on this and that, talking and talking like crazed parrots as they went. No one waited to hear what the next person had to say.

They had passed all the farms belonging to the Asaba people and were beginning to come upon those belonging to the Ibuza people, full of thousands of yam plants each with their delicate stems coiled carefully round and round a planted stick. There were also farms for cassava, with stronger stems and small leaves. They started to meet early farmers, some of whom held pieces of burning wood which they swung this way and that way to keep the glow alive until they reached their farms and could start their fires there.

When the women reached the little Atakpo stream, they rested on its bank. Some cupped water in their hands and gulped it down thirstily.

"Let us go down there and have a bath," Ogugua invited.

69

"With all these people watching?" asked the bewildered Aku-nna.

"You are turning out to be a very sly person, my cousin. What are you hiding? Have you got three breasts or something?"

Aku-nna knew that was not her problem, but she also knew that it would take an earthquake to force her to strip herself here the way her cousin was doing.

"What about all those men on their way to farm?" she whispered to Ogugua. "They are looking at you, and what if the teacher and his friend are still lurking in the bush waiting to see us naked, What of that?" she finished, glad that she had made her point.

Her words simply made her cousin laugh. "It is good that you have come home. You don't know anything at all. The teacher has seen scores and scores of naked women having baths. Why should your particular body be more interesting than the others? And, what's more, he has had lots of mistresses and girlfriends. Just take care. . . ." Ogugua swam away from her cousin, wondering whether they were going to be friends after all. Just because she came from Lagos and spoke quietly, men seemed to like her. She swam back to where Aku-nna was sitting on the damp wild grass of the bank, cooling her tired feet in the slow moving river.

"You must be very careful. That man, that teacher — he's not one of us, you know. No decent girl from a good Ibuza family is allowed to associate with him. My father would rather see his daughter dead than allow such a friendship."

"Why? What has he done? Why is he not one of us? Isn't his family from this town?"

Ogugua burst out laughing once more, then swam away again into the dark part of the river, leaving her cousin muddled in mind. Aku-nna was beginning to hate these outbursts of laughter. What should it matter if the teacher was one of them or not? All she would need from him was to get her certificate. She thought it over to herself; she was disturbed by what Ogugua had said, even though eventually she tried to push it out of her mind. She must ask her mother about it sometime.

They arrived home when the sun was just halfway to noon. It promised to be another hot day though at that time of the morning the temperature was quite bearable, with a wind blowing from the many small streams and rustling among the leaves of the huge tropical trees. Okonkwo had not yet gone to the farm. The teacher and his friend Okine had forewarned him, when they delivered Nna-nndo, that the rest of his brother's family were on their way. He quickly changed his loin cloth and put on a dirty smoky one, then sat on the bare floor and started to wail, as if his brother had only just died. Other men who by that time had not left for the farm were quick to discover what the crying was about and join Okonkwo. Some gunpowder was fired into the air, and that day became a day of mourning, a holiday.

It was with this atmosphere of renewed mourning that Ma Blackie and her helpers were greeted. As they neared the village, the women stopped talking and began to cry out the praise names of Ezekiel Odia.

"Who married his wife in the church?" they asked. "Who spoilt his children with riches? . . . Who was a hard-working man?" Who did this and who did that — on and on they went, singing and weeping at the same time.

It was a surprising change, that these women who less than fiive minutes previously had been discussing the latest cloth designs should suddenly be so grief-stricken. When even Ogugua began to cry, Aku-nna had to do likewise. If what they did in Ibuza was to laugh one minute and howl the next, then she might as well join in. After all, she was going to be one of them.

Young men got together and in less than two hours erected the hut in which Ma Blackie was to stay and mourn for her dead husband for nine full moons. The length of mourning was longer than the usual seven moons because Ezekiel Odia, to ensure that his wife would always be his, had taken the precaution of cutting a lock of hair from Ma Blackie's head and keeping it as evidence. Once a man had taken this step, his wife could never leave him, for to do so would be to commit an abomination; and such a woman, if the husband died, must mourn for nine moons. So testing was this period for a widow that, before it was over, she might herself die and this would be treated as a clear indication that she had been responsible for her husband's death.

Ma Blackie was to remain alone in this special hut; not until the months of mourning were over could she visit people in their homes. She must never have a bath. No pair of scissors nor comb must touch her hair. She must wear continually the same old smoked rags. The fact that she had come dressed in black cotton had caused much controversy and the women in the family were

71

divided over the issue. Some said Ma Blackie could keep and wear these clothes as well during her mourning period, some insisted that she should not.

"Is she courting for a new husband while in mourning?" demanded the latter group. "It is fitting that she should wear only rags."

The long argument was settled by Okonkwo, the head of the family, who bore the Alo title but had ambitions for the higher honours of the *Eze* title which could be his as soon as he had sufficient money. His sights were already set on his brother's wife, his brother's property, and the bride price his brother's daughter would fetch, and he decided that Ma Blackie should be allowed to have her way.

"Let her wear the black cotton when she feels like it. Let her have a black headtie, too. She was married in church, so why should we let her become infested with lice?"

There was a noticeable hush as everyone realised the message behind this pronouncement. Okonkwo Odia wanted his late brother's wife to stay in the family, to be his fourth wife.

6

Traditions

Ibuza was on the western side of the River Niger, in the area that was later to be referred to as the Mid-West State of Nigeria. However much the politicians might divide and redivide the map on paper, though, the inhabitants of the town remained Ibos. History — the oral records, handed down by word of mouth from one generation to the next — said they had migrated from Isu, a town to the east of the river, and although one could hardly be sure of such claims there was certainly evidence to support them. The traditions, taboos, superstitions and sayings of Ibuza were very similar to those still found at Isu.

These were the same traditions that at that time, in the early fifties, guided and controlled the majority of Ibuza's sons and daughters, even those who left the town to work in white men's jobs. Ma Blackie and her family were no exceptions. Nine months after the death of her husband, a hut was built for her next to Ogugua's mother's, and in time it was there that she was visited at night by Okonkwo. She became his fourth wife.

As the months passed, she counted herself lucky in her children. Aku-nna, now approaching fifteen, was intelligent and a promising beauty. Nna-nndo, though he seemed to enjoy the wild life more than school, was settling down nicely. The little capital Ma had managed to save from her husband's gratuity she invested in palm kernels, for she did not wish to have to carry baskets of akpu to market on her head. Her type of trading was different and less strenuous: she would go to the town of Ogwashi to buy the kernels, have them bagged and sent to Ibuza via the one and only lorry which made that trip. On Nkwo market days the bags were transported to Asaba, and Ma would follow on foot; she sold the kernels to eastern Ibo traders, who would have them reprocessed and exported to England to be used in the manufacture of

73

famous brand-name soaps. The cakes of soap would then be re-imported to Nigeria, and women like Ma Blackie would buy them. The kernels, thus, made a completely circular journey.

Ma Blackie automatically belonged to the élite, for her children attended school, and this was a bone of contention between Okonkwo and his other wives and children. They could stomach Nna-nndo's going to school for he was a boy, and also his father had left over one hundred pounds in savings and had joined a progressive Ibuza group called the Pioneer Association, whose aim was to ensure that on the death of any member the first son of that family would be educated to grammar-school level. So there was nothing Okonkwo could have done to stop Nna-nndo's education; at the very least, the boy would go through secondary school. Okonkwo marvelled a great deal at this — fancy his younger brother having enough foresight to provide so far ahead for his son! It was a lesson to be learned. None of Okonkwo's sons, however, showed any liking for school; school was where you sent the family slaves, they snarled at their father, not a place for the children of a free man, though he knew their objection was really because they were not made of the stuff that school demanded. In the olden days, slaves used to be sent there simply to appease the disapproval of the white missionaries; but later events were to show that it was these same educated slaves who ended up commanding key positions. The very people who might once have been expected to bury free men, to be buried alive with them, now had so much money and power that one would not dare call them the descendants of slaves to their faces. Okonkwo sighed, resigning himself to the inevitable.

"There is nothing I can do about it," he told his eldest son, a youth of twenty.

"Yes, I know you can do nothing about the boy. But what of that thing — what do they call her? — Aku-nna? Why waste money on her?" thundered Iloba. He was a promising farmer, working hard to get a wife, but he knew inside himself that he was nothing more than a farmer.

"I would never do such a foolish thing as to pay for her schooling." Okonkwo was on the defensive. He sighed again; if only Aku-nna was his own daughter. Aloud he reasoned: "Her mother pays for her. And she surely won't be going on to any college. So she only has a few more months of school." Here he gave out a loud guffaw.

His sons could not see what there was to laugh about and were not amused. Iloba even looked at him as though he was beginning to doubt his father's sanity.

"You cannot see beyond your noses," said Okonkwo. " You are too young. Don't you know I hope to become an Obi and take the title one day?" In order to become an Obi and receive the respected *Eze* title, a man must make a big and expensive sacrifice to the gods. Then he was given the red cap those who achieved this rank of chieftancy were entitled to wear, and the occasion was followed by days of heavy feasting and drinking; in times past, a slave would have been killed to mark the lavish celebrations.

"Well, what has that got to do with Aku-nna?" Iloba asked.

"Aku-nna and Ogugua will get married at about the same time. Their bride prices will come to me. You see the trend today, that the educated girls fetch more money."

Now his sons smiled. And so did his young wife who, on the pretext of clearing the goats' droppings, was listening to everything. So Aku-nna might after all really live up to her name and be a "father's wealth"; funny how without realising it one came to fulfil one's parents' expectations. Unfortunately her own father had not lived to share the wealth Aku-nna was bound to bring, but not to worry, Okonkwo was almost a father to her now. His sons were pacified, and wondered to themselves at the cleverness and experience their father had just displayed. He wanted to be an Obi, so he needed more money. Aku-nna had to be allowed to stay in school so that she could be married to a rich man, from one of those newly prosperous families springing up like mushrooms all over Ibuza.

They walked silently to their mother Ngbeke's hut. By the door Iloba volunteered, "It happens everywhere now, you know. Did you not hear that the first doctor we have in this town is going to marry a girl from Ogwashi-ukwu? And that her parents are asking the doctor to pay nearly two hundred pounds for her bride price?"

"What's so special about her that the doctor has to pay such a heavy price?" his brother Osenekwu wanted to know.

"She is a nurse and works in hospitals looking after women who give birth to children. That's all. People who have seen her say she is not particularly beautiful, but they say the doctor loves her."

"Ummm, that may be so, but it is a great deal of money to pay for an ordinary woman." He thought a little and added: "I won't mind if Aku-nna fetches us such a large sum. I could do with some money."

They both laughed as they bent their tall bodies to enter their mother's cave-like hut for their evening meal.

Ngbeke eyed them suspiciously, and asked them point-blank what they had been talking to their father about. "Don't tell me it was not anything important, because I saw you. And the way you two laughed just now tells me there is something brewing."

"It is talk between men," Osenekwu replied pompously, feeling really important and a man at the grand age of seventeen. "Ogugua, bring our food, or is there no meal tonight?"

"There is a meal, but Ogugua is filling my pipe for me," their mother said shortly.

In fact Ogugua was doing nothing. She was sitting on the mud step at the back door, picking her nose, and had seen and heard all that was going on. She had had her own meal, and it was too early to call out to her friends for an evening game but too late to go anywhere by herself. She took the hint from her mother and began to fill her pipe with the tobacco leaf her father had sent that morning. This done, she handed it to her mother and brought a burning stick from the fire at the back of their hut. Her mother puffed, and swallowed some of the soothing tobacco smoke, wagging her foot like a contented dog. Then she frowned in the direction of her sons, who were still talking in low tones, making great show of their secret discussion.

"So my sons have grown so much that I am too stupid to know their thoughts, eh?" She coughed and then laughed bitterly, showing her dark teeth, the result of years of tobacco smoking. "Well, what has your father decided to do about the big Miss in the family?"

"Who is 'the big Miss', and how do you know we were talking about her?" demanded Iloba.

Their mother did not answer immediately. She sucked and swallowed, closed her eyes and opened them again. Then she laughed and coughed, spat out some black saliva and said: "I know because I am the woman who taught your father what a woman tastes like. I disvirgined your father and he disvirgined me. And I gave birth to you. And if he becomes an Obi today, it is me he will be taking to Udo with him. It is me that is going to wear the string anklets. So why should I not know? Ogugua, give your brothers their food. They are hungry."

She looked away from her children, and as if talking to herself said, frowning through the smoke, "Okonkwo is making a mistake. It is wrong to put so much hope on his brother's daughter. He could have sent his own daughters to school if he had thought of all this earlier."

"But, Mother, Aku-nna is like a daughter to him now. In fact, according to native law and custom, she is his daughter. Has our father not slept with her mother?" Iloba cried, forgetting that they were not supposed to let their mother know, since such matters were not for women to discuss. "Has my father not been giving them yams from the time they came from Lagos? How then can you talk so, Mother?"

"Eat your food, my son. You are hungry."

"Aku-nna is going to marry a rich man," said Osenekwu between mouthfuls of pounded yam and egusi soup. He kept on repeating the sentence, as if to convince himself that that was how it would be. Aku-nna was going to marry a rich man and raise the entire Odia family from poverty to wealth.

"Keep quiet, and let me hear some other sound," his mother reprimanded. "Which rich man is she going to marry? The son of a slave who teaches at her school? How are you so sure her mother will allow your father to take all her bride price. You forget that her mother was married in the church. You forget that she was trained by Europeans at Ugwu-Ogba. Oh, you forget many things, my stupid men, you forget many, many things," she finished, like a singer closing with a refrain.

Her sons stared at her. What was she talking about? Ma Blackie could not be just using their father in order to train her weak and spoiled brats, could she? Then Iloba shouted at his mother: "My father and nobody else is going to have that bride price!"

"What about Nna-nndo? The other day his mother said he must go to college. What do you think she will use to send him — cocoyam? She too has her eyes on her daughter's bride price. The new European law will be on her side if she claims the money for her son. So you had better tell you father to think like a man. Since when has he started building castles in the air, for the sake of a skinny girl with nothing to her but large eyes that roam in

77

her head like those of a frightened rat whose skull has been banged on the ground? I don't see any strength in that girl. Can you see her bearing children, that one? Her hips are so narrow, and she has not even started to menstruate yet; we are not even sure yet that she is a woman. Look at your sister — they are of the same age, and she started almost a year ago. Had it not been for the fact that I asked your father to wait until she is fifteen, she could have been married off during the last yam festival. Nobody builds castles in the air about your sister — because she was born here, because she is my daughter, because I don't put her in frocks and teach her how to wag her bottom when she walks, because I do not teach her to mix perfume in the coconut oil she puts on her body. That Aku-nna will come to no good, I tell you. She and her mother are too proud," Ngbeke concluded, now puffing and swallowing harder than ever.

Again her sons stared. They did not see the jealousy in their mother's eyes, but they did know that she was speaking the possible truth. Aku-nna was different. She was not allowed to play rough games in the moonlight. She was not allowed to join in the dance her age group were practising for Christmas. There was a kind of softness about her which spelled peace; she would sit and listen to you for hours and just smile all the time and not say anything. And those books the teacher was always lending her! Yes, their mother was right. Aku-nna would soon be fifteen, was still at school and no menstruation. What kind of a girl was she?

"Mother, do you think that girl might be an *ogbanje*?" Iloba asked then.

His mother sighed with relief; her sons had not noticed the jealousy in her words. She resented Ma Blackie for stealing the show in the family she had helped her husband Okonkwo to build. She had not minded his taking younger women as his wives, but now he had graduated to women who were above him in every respect she felt badly affronted. And that the woman was second-hand stuff like the one they called Blackie was an added insult. After all, had not this Blackie woman received her little education in the house of a kind woman trader who had almost bought her, the way one buys a slave? Ezekiel was stupid to have married her in the first place. Just because she wore perfume and liked to line her eyes with black dye! And that daughter of hers — exactly like the mother.

However, she must hide these feelings from her sons, and she was glad that the idea of Aku-nna being an *ogbanje*, a "living dead", had occurred to Iloba. She had forgotten that that could serve as a valve for her jealousy. She suddenly collected herself, realising that her children were quiet and waiting for an answer.

"Yes, I am sure she is one," she pronounced emphatically. "She is different. Have you ever come across someone who seldom talks? I must speak to her mother about it tomorrow. I fear these girls who are *ogbanje*. They all seem to behave too well, but they are only in this world on contract, and when their time is up they have to go. They all die young, usually at the birth of their first baby. They must die young, because their friends in the other world call them back. I am happy none of my three girls was an *ogbanje*, and that they only give me the type of trouble I can cope with, the trouble I can see. A mother is really in the soup when a daughter gives her these unearthly troubles."

"Can't we save her, Mother?" Iloba asked now, frightened. "After all, she is our sister." Though he was only twenty he had seen many young girls die in childbirth. Their deaths were usually very painful because the girls were invariably between the ages of fourteen and eighteen, the delicate and retiring ones, with not much energy. Now it seemed that their cousin, their sister, was like that. Despite everything Iloba liked Aku-nna, and was proud of her little achievements.

"I suppose it is possible these days," said Ngbeke, "if one can get a powerful witch doctor to take her to the site where the agreement with the spirits was made. It costs a great deal of money. That is what the mother should be worrying about, instead of teaching her to wiggle her bottom in short skirts and letting her talk to the son of Ofulue."

"The son of Ofulue? You mean Chike, the school teacher? But he is the son of slaves, Mother, and he knows his place. Chike is only Aku-nna's teacher. He can't help talking to her, because she is in his class. She couldn't be interested in him to that extent!" Iloba cried, his mouth tasting salty. If this was true, it was the greatest insult that could befall a family like theirs, which had never been tainted with the blood of a foreigner, to say nothing of that of the descendants of slaves.

"I will kill her if this is true," Osenekwu swore to himself.

Ogugua, who had listened without comment to the conversation, felt it was high time she put in a word for her friend. She only sensed that her mother was being unnecessarily spiteful, and her upbringing prevented her remarking on it.

"Chike likes Aku-nna, but that is simply because she wants to learn and he is helping her. He knows his place. Was he not born in this town? Does he not know our custom? Has he not seen his older brothers getting wives from outside Ibuza? Why, they are not even good friends. He tells Aku-nna off in class, in front of all the boys."

"There is no smoke without fire, my children. I hope it is only a rumour. But even if it is, it is best to nip it in the bud."

"We should stop listening to such talk, Mother. It is just malicious gossip. How could a quiet girl like that attract such a learned man like Chike, the headmaster of a whole school . . . and a common slave?"

"We must leave it like that," their mother finalised. "But don't forget they have money. And money buys anything these days."

The boys put on their long evening loin cloths and went out of the hut. It was time for them to visit their sweethearts.

Ngbeke had said that there was never smoke without fire, and she was right. Chike was falling in love with his fifteen-year-old pupil without knowing it; even had it occurred to him what was happening he was powerless to stop the process. He had never seen a girl so dependent, so unsure of herself, so afraid of her own people.

The CMS school where Chike Ofulue was head teacher served as a church as well. The building was long, whitened with clay, but the window shutters were darkened with black *uli* leaves. The windows were circular and the doors were very small, and the roof was artistically covered with *akanya* leaves.

The first thing that struck Aku-nna and her brother as rather odd was the size of the boys. These boys were certainly not boys any more: most of them were men. There were only three girls in the whole school and, as she was later to discover, she was the oldest of them and in the highest class. On that first day, she clung to her school bag for reassurance.

"Hello," a low voice cooed just behind her ear.

She was so startled that she almost jumped. She had been pre-occupied watching just in front of her a young man climbing a

80

rather shaky clay construction and trying to reach a bell. It was the first time she had seen a bell-ringer, and she was marvelling at his agility when the hello came. Turning her head, Aku-nna saw that the salutation was from the teacher. Since they met on her first day in Ibuza she had seen him several times, once at the church where he was leading the choir and another time when he had been rushing to his farm and she was washing some clothes at the Atakpo stream.

"Good morning, sir."

She was about to shy her way into the midst of the schoolboys standing about in groups of twos and threes and talking among themselves, when he stopped her with: "What do you think of this school? I know it must seem different from any of the schools you have seen before."

He was right there. She had never seen a school covered with leaves, neither had she seen a man swinging up and down with each ding-dong of the bell, just like a monkey. She smiled politely, to avoid having to say anything. The teacher smiled too and left her, for the bell had stopped and the whole school was beginning to congregate on the green grass.

They had a short service in the open air. The teacher, in his white shorts and shirt and his perfectly knotted black tie with white diagonal lines on it, said all the prayers that were necessary. The white man who was the head of the mission stood aside, looking very old and uncomfortable in his long white robe; the sun was already out and the poor white man, now coffee-coloured, was wiping his brow as he stood there under one of the innumerable mango trees scattered about the large compound, singing in his shaky voice as he took part in the service.

When the time came for the announcements, the white man spoke in a strange sort of dialect which he seemed to think was Ibo. He did not realise that his audience was having so much difficulty in understanding him that it would have been better if he had simply addressed them in English. But that would have offended the Right Reverend Osborne, who had come all the way from Oxford in England and had spent many long years learning the Ibo language. He welcomed them all back after the holidays and said he hoped they would work even harder than they had the term before. He hoped that everybody's family was enjoying the best of health, and begged each member of the school to

81

convey his own personal greetings and blessings to their mothers and fathers and cousins and friends. The whole school cheered. Reverend Osborne had captured the African spirit all right, after all.

Aku-nna and Nna-nndo soon grew accustomed to things at Ibuza, learning in school the European ways of living and coming home to be faced with the countless and unchanging traditions of their own people. Yet they were like helpless fishes caught in a net; they could not as it were go back into the sea, for they were trapped fast, and yet they were still alive because the fisherman was busy debating within himself whether it was worth killing them to take home, seeing as they were such small fry.

One or two things were certain to Aku-nna. She had not only lost a father, she had also lost a mother. Ma Blackie found herself so immersed in the Okonkwo family politics, and in making ends meet, that she seldom had time to ask how the world was with her daughter. Aku-nna realised this, and did not allow herself to appear a nuisance. Several times, in anger, Ma Blackie had asked her to show her another girl in the whole of Ibuza who was without a father and still able to continue her schooling. There were few girls who were so fortunate. This knowledge drove Aku-nna more and more into herself until, in deed rather than in words, Chike Ofulue told her that she was valued, treasured and loved.

7

The Slaves

"We are all equal in the sight of the Lord." This statement was hammered into Chike's ears by the Reverend Osborne right from the time the boy could understand the English language.

Chike had heard his mother mention occasionally that his grandmother had been a princess who was captured from Ubulu-ukwu, a town only fifteen miles from Ibuza, in the days where there were no roads but only footpaths used by warriors. She was very beautiful and her master Obi Ofulue decided not to sell her on but to buy a man slave to keep her company. By the time her master died and she had to be buried alive with him, she had already borne four sons and two daughters. The girls were sold, but the rightful son of Ofulue retained all the boys. Soon it became illegal to sell slaves; Ofulue, not wanting to lose face with these Europeans who suddenly stopped buying slaves and turned into missionaries instead, preaching of a kind of God of whom he had never heard, decided to send the Ofulue men slaves to them. Most of the slaves whom the missionaries took in were to become the first teachers, headmasters, and later their children became the first doctors and lawyers in many Ibo towns.

The lasting effects of such old-fashioned ideas about slavery were not new to Chike; he had heard it all before and was not too concerned about it. He was handsome and though women knew that he came from an *"oshu"* family, a slave family, they pretended not to see it. Had not his family produced many professional men? Did not his half-brothers and sisters own the biggest and longest cars the town of Ibuza had ever seen? In fact, he looked down on most of the local girls. Yes, he had slept with lots of them in his late teens, and even still had a few mistresses among the younger wives of many old chiefs. His conscience did not worry him on that score, for these wives were still in the flush of girlhood yet tied to ageing husbands who above all prided themselves on providing enough yam to fill their spouses' bellies. If they suspected that their wives needed more than yams to satisfy them, they were not talking. If they were aware that half the numbers of children being born and saddled with their name were not theirs, they knew better than to raise a scandal. In Ibuza, every young man was entitled to his fun.

The blame usually went to the girls. A girl who had had adventures before marriage was never respected in her new home; everyone in the village would know about her past, especially if she was unfortunate enough to be married to an egocentric man. There were men who would go about raping young virgins of thirteen and fourteen, and still expect the women they married to be as chaste as flower buds. And even such wives were soon taught evil ways; they might bear the insults and humiliation for a while, perhaps until their first children were born, but then they too grew wings. For it was regarded as shameful for a man no longer to be able to satisfy his wife sexually; rather than admit it, he would go out of his way to pay the bride prices of many more, in order to enhance his masculine image. An impotent man was very rare in Ibuza, and the few that existed were no more than living dead.

Chike's parents knew of his indulgencies, but did not try to curb him; he had the money and freedom to choose his own pleasures. So he was taken by surprise when one evening his father solemnly called him into their sitting-room, which was furnished like some tropical Victorian parlour, with stiff leather chairs, colourful cane window blinds and a mighty fan. The senior Ofulue was himself a teacher, though now retired; he had four wives all from nearby towns, and on the whole had led a very enviable life. The people of Ibuza would never forgive him for being so prosperous. They would never forgive him for having illustrious children, through whom the existence of a small town like theirs was being made known to the rest of Nigeria. Although he was a member of the Native Administration the people had never allowed him to become a chief; for, they reasoned, the day a slave becomes a chief in this town, then we know that our end is near. Ofulue was amused by it all; he did not intend to ask the people of Ibuza to bend over backwards for his sake. His children taught in their schools, his children treated their old people free in the hospitals. Yet they were still slaves, *oshu*.

Now he cautioned Chike. "I went to school with Ezekiel Odia. I was a senior when he was still learning his ABC. I would not like a son of mine to bring shame on his only daughter. I saw the way you were looking at her in church — everybody noticed it. But I beg you not to spoil the girl."

Chike was taken aback; he thought he had succeeded in keeping his feelings under lock and key. He had hoped people would think he regarded Aku-nna as just another pupil. He had not even spoken to the girl outside his lessons. But he had to say something to his father, if only to put his mind at rest. He thought hard, then he said:

"I do care for her. She is so alone. But I would not spoil her — how can a man spoil an angel?" His voice was choking with emotion.

Ofulue looked at his son for a long while, then pointedly reminded him that he would have to work hard at his studies to get into university in the coming year.

Anger threatened inside Chike and he stared at his father with eyes that almost began to have hatred in them. How could his own father say such a hurtful thing when he knew full well what had happened — that Chike had all the university entrance requirements and yet some reason or other had been found to refuse him a Federal Scholarship? It had been painful enough at the time, so much so that had it not been for love of his mother, sisters and little brothers Chike would gladly have left Ibuza for some town where no one would ever know of him. He still felt sore thinking about it, and now his father was rubbing it in. Why? To press home the fact that his sons by other women had gone through their university careers without costing their father anything?

"I was not considered good enough for a scholarship," he snapped resentfully.

"I know that," his father replied slowly, as though he intended to help Chike to go on being sorry for himself. "But you have chosen an odd course. Sociology." He pronounced the word like a German: sokiologgy. "Maybe the examiners have never heard of it. I am not quite sure myself what you aim to become after this sociology course. An office worker? A politician? We have too many politicians already, and anyway you don't need a university degree to be a good politician. Any fool can be a politician; you just have to teach yourself how to tell convincing lies like a gentleman, that's all. Can't you change your subject?" he asked, after a pause.

Chike stared vacantly at the whitewashed walls on which were nailed many family photographs. He had seen these pictures many times before, but just this evening they seemed to loom larger than life. So his father wanted him to be a doctor or a lawyer or an engineer — the famous trinity careers of the Nigerian élite. It was perfectly all right to refer to "my son the lawyer", "my son the doctor" or "my son the engineer", but whoever heard of anyone in his right senses saying proudly "my son the sociologist"?

"I don't want to change, Father. We cannot all be doctors. There is a great deal you learn when you are a sociologist," was Chike's defence of his chosen profession.

"You must apply again this year. Even if you are not given the scholarship you want, I will pay the university fees," his father said, looking away from his son like a shy woman would.

Chike was beginning to see the light. So he was to be bribed out of Ibuza. What other reason could there be behind his father's offer? It was against his policy to pay for higher education for any of his children, simply because there were so many of them. To be fair to all his wives, he gave every child the opportunity of good education up to school certificate level; the girls were not particularly encouraged but he never said no to any of his daughters who gained admission to grammar school or to a teacher training college. It was obvious that his father wanted him out of town because he thought he was getting involved with Aku-nna. He felt angry again.

"Is she not a girl to be married some day?" he demanded in harsh tones.

He had gone too far, and he knew it. His father had grown fat, since his retirement; his movements had become not only slow but majestic, commanding of respect. Chike watched the folds of fat at the back of his neck and they now seemed to be swelling, like an African snail coming out of its shell. And also like a snail, the back of his father's neck was very black; his hair had gone grey and so he dyed his shaven head with Morgan's Pomade, which he applied so liberally that it went far beyond his hairline. The eyes he turned towards his son were like ripe palm kernels. He had a small voice, and talked very little, and now when he spoke it was like the sound of a goat bleating in pain as it was about to be slaughtered for a festival.

"You will leave that girl alone or . . . or. . . ." He did not complete the sentence. He waved his hand as though at an obnoxious fly that had just come from perching on excrement. "Out of my sight!"

Chike left his father, more puzzled than ever. It was a Sunday, and he did not know how he survived the night.

It is said that stolen water is sweet. Maybe Chike would have outgrown Aku-nna and maybe she would come to regard anything there might be between them as mere childish infatuation, if the adults had just left them alone. For her it was always, "Don't get yourself mixed up with that teacher. You see how all the girls at his school always pass their exams? He never canes them, like the Catholic Fathers did." Don't do this, don't do that. It was all don'ts, and to Aku-nna the cautions became everyday trivia, not worth remembering and good simply for ignoring. Any warning voices she might hear in herself were too indistinct to be effective. For one thing, Aku-nna did not know, and no one told her, what they were warning against. Even her cousins seemed too apprehensive to be specific. All they did was be watchful and make vague hints; only a madman would call another man "oshu" to his face. This was the age of the white man's law. The white man had come to stay, and this culture seemed to be gaining ground; so if you did not want trouble for yourself or your family, you abided by the laws of the white man.

Chike tried as much as possible to push his private problems out of his mind and to concentrate on coaching his pupils for their coming examination. He tried to avoid talking directly to Aku-nna throughout that Monday. Towards the end of the afternoon, however, he asked the pupils to recite the reasons for the European scramble for Africa in the eighteenth century. When it came to Aku-nna's turn, it seemed that she had forgotten them all. Chike gave her every possible hint and prompting — that by that time quinine had been discovered, that the slave trade was then a paying enterprise, that Africa which had previously been the white man's graveyard was by then becoming his paradise. . . .

Still Aku-nna looked blank.

"Look, are you asleep?" Chike shouted. "Didn't you revise your notes at all at the weekend? How am I supposed to help you if all you are going to do is stand there and stare at me?"

The others in the class found this a welcome diversion, and they started to heckle and jeer. For once Chike forgot them and could see only his father, in his mind's eye, telling him to leave the girl alone. But how could one leave alone another human being who was metaphorically drowning? If he did not interfere in her life, only the gods in hell could tell where she would be bundled in a year or two, just to satisfy the ambition of her uncle. Chike told himself that what he felt for the girl was pity; he did not question whether one usually got annoyed and shouted at someone one was sorry for. If it occurred to him that you might sometimes lose your temper with a person you loved, he did not now appear to give it much thought.

"Does that mean you can't even remember one reason for the scramble for Africa?" His voice was low and charged with suppressed exasperation. He came nearer, mopping the sweat from his brow, for it was a very hot day.

"I did not have time to learn my notes last night, because, because. . . ."

"Because she was entertaining her boyfriends," a voice like a frog's croaked from behind her. The boys all laughed. Aku-nna burst into tears. The laughter grew louder than ever.

Chike banged the desk in front of Aku-nna with so much force that the whole class immediately became silent. He told them that he was not tolerating such loose behaviour from them. He ordered the boy who had made the stupid remark about Aku-nna to stand up, and told him he should be ashamed of himself for making such an irresponsible statement. The boy was grinning from ear to ear, though his lips were trembling, for he sensed danger in the voice of the man he knew so well. The defiant grin was simply to boost his ego. The other boys looked away, knowing better than to join him.

Aku-nna had not stopped crying.

"What is the matter, then?" Chike asked, in a voice so soft that it was apparent it was meant for her ears alone. She sniffed into her scarf and did not reply. "You are excused," he said quietly to her, moving away to the front of the class to continue the lesson as though nothing had happened.

Aku-nna mumbled her thanks and stumbled out, colliding with almost everything and everybody on her way. What was the matter with her? She wondered as much as any of them. She was upset about something, that was clear, but she herself could not identify what it was that was unsettling her.

She stopped trying to work it out, and simply lumped herself at the foot of an orange tree at the far end of the school field, where she could not easily be seen, and gave way to glorious grief. Tears poured down her face in plenty, like rain water, and she did not attempt to check them. Was she not alone, by herself, enjoying this luxurious moment of sweet self-pity? Somewhere in the distance the school bell rang, as if from another world, but she ignored it, completely encapsulated as she was by the sur-rounding orange trees. She watched and listened to a group of chattering birds who appeared to feel safe and undisturbed by her presence. She noticed that they were building a nest. Each bird brought a strand of palm leaf, clutching it preciously in its beak then laying it down artistically in the right place. To Aku-nna's surprise, a small bowl-like basket structure was soon formed. She was enthralled by the obvious enjoyment with which they worked. The nest in the tree very near to where she was sitting was being built by two birds; sweethearts, perhaps. Their happiness, their ability to communicate so intimately with one another, brought home to her more vividly her predicament.

She had lost her father. Her mother was, literally, lost to her, so deeply was Ma engulfed in the affairs of Okonkwo's household; it was difficult sometimes to remember that she had been married to Aku-nna's father. Her brother was too young, too spoilt, to be any consolation to her. As a boy, and as the heir of the Ezekiel Odia branch of the family, he was allowed to do what he liked, and anyway he was too childish to be trusted. Her cousin Ogugua was friendly but gullible, and if told any secrets would surely repeat them, not just word for word but adequately spiced by her own imagination. It came to Aku-nna clearly now that she was com-pletely alone. She sat there, dry-eyed now, following the move-ments of the birds without actually seeing them, absorbed in her own troubled thoughts.

"Aku-nna, I think you need your certificate more than anybody in the class, don't you?" She looked up in the direction of the

89

voice to see Chike standing there, a disturbed expression on his face. "If you are going to sit there just dreaming all your life away you will fail the examination, and you know as well as I do that your people would never let you sit it again."

Aku-nna could say nothing to defend herself. She merely gazed at him there, standing tall and thin, his tamed curls almost touching the orange tree branches. He must have been playing football with the boys, for his open-necked shirt revealed the damp hairs clinging on his moist chest; his white sleeves were rolled up to his elbows and his shorts were crumpled. She did not bother to get up from the root of the tree where she sat. She diverted her gaze to his white plimsolls, the laces of which were tied like bows.

"What was the matter with you in class?" he asked, this time sounding not like a teacher but like someone who really cared.

Something in his voice made her look up. How could she explain that she felt alone among her own relatives? How could she tell him that she herself was not capable of putting into words what it was that ailed her so? She took refuge in tears once more. Chike seemed to grow larger and larger, and his head came more into her focus. She looked straight into the open distance and let the tears fall on her cheeks, not bothering to wipe them away. Without saying anything more, he sat beside her on the root of the orange tree.

Near their feet, a group of brown ants was winding its way into a tiny hole. They both watched in silence the perfect line the ants made. No single ant deviated from the main column, all followed the same route one after the other, as if at the command of a power invisible. Each was carrying a little white substance in its mouth which seemed to be food of some sort, bearing the particles into their hole. Absentmindedly, Chike placed a dried orange leaf in their path, blocking their way.

Aku-nna looked up at him and asked in a watery voice: "Why did you do that? They will lose their way."

"No, they won't," he replied, removing the leaf from the ants' track. The ants quickly reformed and carried on with their business as if nothing had happened.

"Why do they follow one another like that?"

"Because each ant would be lost if it did not follow the footsteps of those in front, those who have gone on that very path before." He stopped short. Was that what his father was trying to tell him the night before? That he should forget this girl and let custom and tradition take their course? He was finding that impossible to do. He noticed that her tears had stopped; he felt she needed reassurance, so he said aloud: "I shall help you pass that examination, if it is the last thing I do before I leave this horrible town."

"Leave it? Where are you going?" The disappointment and expectancy in her voice was such that it was transparent to him that she cared.

"University," he said brusquely, taking hold of the left hand she rested at one side of her and pulling her up with a rather rough jerk.

As she stood, she felt a slight pain in her back and noted that her skin was going moist. She felt peculiar somehow, and was sure she was shivering even though the day was so warm.

"Do you want me to go?" he asked.

She shook her head; no, she did not want him to go. But should she tell him that ever since the first day she had met him on his new bicycle she had not stopped thinking of him, seeing him in her mind's eye, feeling so much happiness just at the sound of his voice, wanting to touch him, yearning to assure him that all would be well when the boys in the class proved particularly difficut? How could she tell him that she needed him, that she was all alone in this world, without appearing cheap and badly brought up? She was sure people would say she was just attracted by the big houses and cars his family had; but those same people would insist that he was an *osu*, the son of a common slave. But if he left, left her here alone in this town, she would be heartbroken. She would be lost, like the ants without their tracks. If she disobeyed her mother and uncle, and if in future Chike became nasty and started to beat her — as most Ibuza men seemed to beat their women — then nobody would put in a kind word for her. They would say to her, "Why did you get involved with an *osu* in the first place? These slaves do not know how to treat the sons and daughters of free men. It is like giving gold to a pig — it would not know what to do with it." Her eyes mirrored her thoughts and she felt like crying again. He searched her upturned eyes, noticing their largeness, the loneliness in them and the tears, not very far away.

"Why are you so unhappy? Why do you cry so much about

91

everything? I'd like to make sure that you only cry out of happiness, not sadness. Now we must go back to the class. It's time for singing. You can cry while the others sing, and the sound will be all the more melodious."

He indicated to her to go ahead of him, so that the rest of the school would not see them emerging from that corner together. At the same time he said, "I must come and see your mother this evening about your homework." Then he suddenly stopped, and called out sharply, "Aku-nna! You are bleeding, there is blood on your dress . . . Aku-nna."

She swirled round quickly, looked and saw that there was blood smeared on a part of the hem of her dress. At first she was frightened, thinking that she had hurt herself. Then common sense took over, and she knew what was happening to her. She had heard about it from her friends so many times, she had seen it happen to many women, she had been told about it often by her mother and she knew the responsibility that went with it. She was now fully grown. She could be married away, she could be kidnapped, a lock of her hair could be cut by any man to make her his wife forever. All at once she was seized by a severe cramp; her feet left like giving way, small pains like needles shot in her back and she could feel something warm running down her legs. What should she do now — run, run as far as possible from this man, and never let him see her again? She was intensely annoyed by his presence. How dare he see her in this shameful state? But would it have been any better if her mother or one of those boys had been the first to know?

He came closer to her, not caring whether they were seen or not. He wanted to marry this girl, even if it meant breaking all the laws of Ibuza. As he held her to his clammy chest, her body shook, from fear and from something else inside her which she could not name. He stroked the perspiration from her forehead, dipped his nose into her short curls.

"The first time?"

"Yes." Her reply was a whisper.

It seemed that they stood there for a long time. He did not want her to go, and she herself did not want to go. Who else could she talk to? Then the cramp came again and she felt weak, longing for a place to lie down. She told him that she felt funny, and she could feel his heart beating fast. It was a mutual distress.

"You wait here," he said, letting her go gently. "I'll get you something from the first-aid kit. Sit down, where you were before. I shall not be long."

She obeyed, though the root of the tree was as hard as iron, and she felt so sore that she could have cried out. But she allowed him to take over; he seemed more experienced than she was. How could he help but know all about it, after having read so many books, having seen all his sisters go through the same experience so many times until he had become fed up with the whole atmosphere of it and built himself a small bachelor cottage close to his father's big house?

He soon returned. She did not see him coming, because she was thinking and her eyes were closed. What would happen now? Would her people stop her going to school? The only thing she could do was to hide it, but how could she? The Ibuza women usually used rags which they changed frequently for freshness and washed several times a day — where would she dry hers without being seen? And when a woman was unclean, she must not go to the stream, she must not enter a household where the man of the family had either the *"Eze"* or *"Alo"* title — her uncle Okonkwo had the latter; if she went into such a house, the head of the family would die and the oracle would discover who the culprit was. She might not be killed in broad daylight, but Ibuza people had ways, psychological measures, to eliminate those who committed the abominable *alu*.

Chike handed her two white tablets and a glass of water. He gave her his big woollen jumper which he wore on cold mornings when the Harmattan wind blew and which he had left with the Osbornes. Then, watching her swallow the water, he asked, "Akum . . . can you keep quiet about this? Don't tell anyone yet, not till after the exam."

Her confusion was giving way to a kind of mild joy, especially as she noticed that Chike had called her Akum, meaning "my wealth". She did not mind belonging to him and being his wealth; she would like to be owned by a man like Chike. If only people would stop calling him a slave behind his back. If only people did not object so much. . . .

"How will I hide it?" she asked. "I sleep in the same hut as my mother, and she is bound to know."

He looked away. What would be the point of pretending to this

93

innocent that he did not know much about women?

"You forget that my brother is a doctor, and I have seen what European women use in these cases. After school, I will go down to Onitsha and buy you a packet. You must hide it, and keep it safe and clean. I shall wrap it up just like a book so your mother will not know. Go home now. I shall tell your brother that you have a headache. And please make sure that your dress is covered by that jumper." He could not see her eyes, for they were lowered; he told her softly not to worry about anything. And he told her one more thing: he said, "I love you," and then walked away.

There was nothing for her to do but to go home. The pain in her back had lessened, thanks to the tablets. She wondered if this was the way she would feel every month for the rest of her life. She hated herself now. Messy and smelly. She could have stood the messiness but for this horrid backache and her legs going crampy. She felt she would not dare to laugh out loud, or else the blood would gush out. She gave a gentle cough to test herself, and the effect was the same. She would have to rush home, before people began to return from the markets and farms.

By the time she had walked the mile or so home the relief of the tablets had worn off. Her head throbbed in sympathy with her depression. She could not lie down straight away for she felt unclean. She found a little water in their jar and used it to wash herself; her brother would raise a row when he came and found that there was none left, but she was too ill to care. Oh, if only there were a magic hand to rub her waist, or something really hot to wrap round it. How it hurt her! She lay on the mud couch and drifted into a fitful sleep.

She woke up at the sound of her name. Nna-nndo was calling her from the doorway, asking her what the matter was this time. She was always ill, he complained. He spared her half a second to enquire, "Did you tell the teacher that you were ill?"

"Yes, I became ill in class." Aku-nna wished very much that her brother would take himself away to wherever boys of his age went at that time of the day.

He grunted and went straight to the water pot. It had been a very hot afternoon and he was thirsty. He dipped inside with a tin cup for a long while but came up with not a drop of water. With every effort he made his anger mounted.

94

"What's happened to the water? This pot was almost full this morning before we left for school. What's happened to all of it?" Nna-nndo flung the tin cup down on the mud floor.

Maybe if Aku-nna had kept quiet and pretended not to know anything about it, her brother would have let the matter be. But human conscience always lets one down when one least expects it, and she felt it was her duty to offer some explanation.

"Perhaps Mother used it before she left for Abuano market." It was a very unconvincing lie. What would their mother be doing with half a pot full of water when she knew she would be going to pass the Oboshi stream on her way? Women did not wash their clothes at home; and unless they were very ill they did not bath in the hut, except that is for the few enlightened ones who felt like washing themselves down at those times when they were considered unclean and it was taboo to go to the stream.

Nna-nndo came nearer to her and hissed, "Liar! Mother left the house before we did, in case you have forgotten, you *ogbanje* liar. It's about time you decided whether you are going to stay alive with us or die. Today foot, tomorrow head — all on you alone! And another thing, if you think I am going to that stream just to satisfy a sickly sister you'll have to think again, because I'm not going, and that is a fact. What did you do with the water anyway?"

She did not answer the last question; and he, thank goodness, did not press for a reply. He started a fire, and pushed in a piece of yam left over from the evening meal the night before. The smoke from the wood curled round and round the hut and the smell of cooking filled the air. It was the type of fresh yam smell that normally made her mouth water like that of a hungry dog, but today it revolted her. The yam was soon done, and she could hear her brother scraping off the burnt parts and chewing the good part, gnashing his teeth like a squirrel cracking nuts. The hot yam accentuated his thirst. He stated again that he was not going to the stream, even if he choked with thirst. But he knew what he was doing to do: he would borrow a bottle of water from his friend Dumebi's house. He went out, yam in one hand and an empty green beer bottle in the other. Unfortunately for him, Dumebi's mother was at home and wanted to know why he could not go and fetch some water from the stream for his sister and mother to cook with. No, she was not going to give him any;

the Atakpo stream was there for anyone who made the effort. She lamented the fate of the future generation. She wondered what the world was coming to. A twelve-year-old boy begging for water like an old woman!

Nna-nndo stared for a second at her tobacco-stained mouth. It was as dark as the waterless well in the village of Ogboli, a well that was so dark that rumour had it ghosts and evil spirits feasted there. He was certain the Dumebi's mother's mouth could also accommodate the vilest spirit of hell. He walked away very quickly, throwing aside the rest of his yam. His throat was too dry to enjoy it. When he returned to their hut he did not talk to his sister, but went straight to where their mother put the gourds to dry out by the fireplace and, after much noisy and angry banging, chose the smallest one. He took out his fishing rod, and it was clear he was going down to the stream. Aku-nna silently thanked her stars.

The moon that night was round and untarnished. Its brilliance found its way through the crevices of huts and shone right inside, forming beautiful yellow patterns on the mud floors of the dark rooms. With the little water Nna-nndo fetched from the stream, Aku-nna managed to cook for him and their mother. Then she went to lie down again, listening to all their neighbours pounding yams for the evening meals. She must have drifted off into a tired sleep for she almost jumped at the pounding on their heavy wooden door. Her fear lessened when she realised that it was only her cousin, Ogugua.

"Don't tell me you are reading in that darkness, with no light?" she asked, stepping inside carefully so as not to collide with anything, for despite the bright moonlight outside it had become very gloomy in the hut. "What's the matter with you? Are you sick? Have you forgotten that we are meant to go and meet our mothers coming back from Abuano and help them carry their market buys?"

There were too many questions and Aku-nna did not know which one to answer first. "I don't feel well. Please take some of my mother's things for her. I am not too bad, it's just that I can't go." She got up and filled the earthenware lamp with palm oil and lit it.

In the pale glow of light now in the room Ogugua studied her and diagnosed, "It's a headache. I can see it in your eyes. They are very red." She did not stay long, for as she said she was late already, and if her mother had already passed Ogbewele when she met her, there would be a row. She promised to help Aku-nna's mother as well and would persuade their age-group friend Obiageli to do the same.

Ogugua hurried out, calling to the others at the top of her voice to leave their food; the moon was out and their poor mothers were on their way home from Abuano. Ogugua was a native Ibuza girl who would one day be able to hold her own in her husband's house, Aku-nna thought as she heard her voice in the distance.

She did not risk lying down again. Her mother would soon be back and then the boys who came to their hut for night games would begin trooping in. Their custom allowed this. Boys would come into your mother's hut and play at squeezing a girl's breasts until they hurt; the girl was supposed to try as much as possible to ward them off and not be bad-tempered about it. So long as it was done inside the hut where an adult was near, and so long as the girl did not let the boy go too far, it was not frowned on. Some girls did eventually marry their early sweethearts, but in most cases the boys were either too young to afford the bride price or were not ready for marriage. They usually stood by and watched their first loves married off to men old enough to be their fathers.

Aku-nna was spreading out on the mud couch a smooth mat made in Sierra Leone, which Ma had brought with them from Lagos, when a gentle knock on the door stopped her. She invited whoever it was to enter.

Chike came inside.

He had bought her everything she needed, and even a small book to explain it all to her. He sat beside her on the couch and put his arm close round her. He remarked that she was still hot, and she explained that it was through cooking at the fire. He touched her breasts, the way a suitor might, not the way the rough boys squeezed them just for fun. Aku-nna felt her body going funny and playing some tricks on her she did not know. She was frightened of the teacher now, for he seemed to be making her touch his front, which was hardening like the tree root on which she had sat that afternoon. He saw her eyes clouding, and knew that she was indeed growing into a young woman. He held her like that and asked her what she thought they should do.

97

"Tell my people that you want to marry me," she said, her voice faint and whispery.

He suddenly abandoned his gentleness and his soft hands fondled her more desperately. She gave a subdued cry, and he said he was sorry, but couldn't she see that they would never allow it? Had she not heard that his ancestors were slaves and had never been born in this land? Did she think it was a joke. . . .?

She covered his mouth with her hand, not knowing where the boldness which was working inside her came from. "There is no other person for me in this world, Chike. I don't even know anyone else — I always say the wrong thing, do the wrong thing. You are the only person I know who I am not afraid of. So don't say that. . . ."

He did not know what else to do but to start kissing her the way Europeans did in films. Aku-nna knew one was supposed to like being kissed but she did not know how to enjoy it. She had read in old copies of *True Romances* that kissing was meant to do something to a girl. Well, it had done nothing for her, but she let him have his play. All she wanted was to make him happy, to make him realise that his being an outcast did not matter to her. The one thing that bothered her was that she had also heard from somewhere that kissing caused tuberculosis, but she did not want to ask him about that now, for what was the point? She had already been kissed so much that when he let her go she was breathless; so if she was going to catch T.B. it was too late to recoil.

"You will always be mine," he said into her ear, his voice so thick that she could swear it was coming from some other man lurking in the corner.

She was worried about what he might do next, so she stood up, telling him that her mother would be back soon. He agreed that he should go and asked her to keep it all to herself. Yes, she could show her mother the two giant tins of Ovaltine he had bought, but nothing else. There was no time for further talk for they could hear the buzz of voices coming close. It would be bad manners for him to leave yet, so he waited to welcome Ma Blackie and Nna-nndo home.

His pupil had been taken ill in class, he explained, so he had come to see how she was; he had not realised Ma Blackie had gone to market or he would have come much later. Ma Blackie showed some concern over her daughter and pointed out that maybe the Ibuza air did not agree with her; she had not been herself since they came from Lagos. The teacher said he had brought a bottle of headache tablets which would make her feel better.

Aku-nna listened with her eyes lowered. She did not dare look up. Her mother might see many things she was not yet prepared to know about her daughter.

Chike bade goodnight to all, and offered to bring her school work the next day if she did not feel up to coming.

Ma Blackie's alarm showed in her voice. "Of course she will be there tomorrow," she said with unnecessary emphasis. She looked from one to the other, and her look warned Chike to mind his step.

He said his goodnight once again. Ma Blackie answered, but Aku-nna did not. So many things had happened to her in one day, so many things about herself which she did not understand.

8

A Kind of Marriage

It was never long before a visitor to Ibuza could tell — from the culture, the traditions, the mode of keeping records, the superstitions — that this was an Ibo town. What was more difficult to make out was whether to classify the people as Christians or pagans. Many people went to church, and about three-quarters of those who did attended the Catholic church, for there was a general belief in Ibuza in things mysterious. The Church Missionary Society service was too plain; the sermon was usually preached by an African, and in most cases an African from their own town, and such sermons did not carry much weight with the faithful of Ibuza. A sermon preached by an Irish Father, full of the mystic incantations that formed part of the rigmarole of Catholicism, imparted to the Ibuza citizens the feeling that they had been spoken to by God Almighty Himself. They might not be able to follow or understand the Latin Mass, but the glamour of the robes of the Reverend Father, the cloying smell of the incense, the Indian-sounding chants, all helped to mystify and convince the ignorant.

There were various different societies in the town, most of them existing for social purposes; but in the main it was one's age group that determined membership. Age groups were created at three-year intervals, each one characterised by an important incident. (Childen born during the civil war would become known as the children of Biafra, and when babies born at that time grow into adolescence they will hold meetings, organise dances, in the big Eke market; they might have special dances which will take years of practice for the Christmases of their youth or the Ifejoiku yam festivals.)

Aku-nna was born at about the time when the River Niger drowned hundreds of young Ibuza girls between the ages of four-

100

teen and eighteen. Most of them had gone to Onitsha on that particular market day to buy clothes for going away to their new husbands' homes, and crossing the river on their way back they were unfortunately overtaken by a storm so violent that nearly all those in the open and unprotected canoes lost their lives. Only one or two of the canoe paddlers survived and that was because, since they lived close to the Niger, they were expert swimmers.

In all nine villages which formed the town of Ibuza these dead girls were mourned for months. Everyone knew, or thought they knew, why these girls had been lost: the River Niger was only claiming back her own. It was a predetermined and fatalistic belief, but it was enough to comfort the bereaved. Their acceptance of the idea that there was nothing anyone could have done to prevent it, the thought that their daughters had been chosen to serve at the court of the beautiful goddess of the river, nullified the pangs of pain to no small extent. After the period of mourning, the story went, many Ibuza women became pregnant, and when most of them subsequently gave birth to girls there was a joyous understanding that the river goddess had given these new baby girls to replace the ones she had taken. That age group became associated with the year the River Niger ate the children of Ibuza — the Ibo people would never say that a victim had drowned but that he or she had been eaten by the river, for underpinning such an event was the belief that every river had a goddess who could do with one or two human sacrifices from time to time.

Aku-nna belonged to this popular age group. This was their fifteenth year, and few of them had yet married though the majority knew that this approaching Christmas would be their last in their fathers' houses. Christmas was a very important time of the year for everyone. Schools were closed and teachers were on holiday. Those who had ventured to other parts of the country usually came home around this time to show off their acquired wealth to their less fortunate relatives who had remained farmers all their lives. Aku-nna's age group were marking the occasion this year with a dance to entertain their people, and there was talk that they would also be going to places like Ubulu-ukwu and Isele Azagba to show off their skills in the intricate steps. So instead of going out to play in the moonlight, or amusing themselves in their mothers' huts with the local youths, they all spent

101

the evenings learning their special *aja* dance.

Because she had been kept busy preparing for her examination, Aku-nna had not taken part in these sessions from the beginning, but now that it was over and there were two weeks to wait before the results were released, she needed to occupy herself with the dance practices, for she was not confident that she would be successful. She realised that she had a good voice, trained by years of singing in the church choir, so the songs were not too difficult to learn with the help of her cousin Ogugua. This break from school was a good opportunity to get to know her new friends more, and Aku-nna was beginning to enjoy it. Her circle of acquaintances widened to include not only Ogugua in a different and more intimate way but also several other girls such as Obiageli, whose grandmother sold a kind of Ibo pudding made from ripe plantain, and Obiajulu, whose father was a wealthy red-cap chief with many wives and very proud daughters.

The dance teacher was a tall man who could be taken for very young, although he was older than he looked, for he was still very slim and without any sagging flesh. He had inherited his first wife and she was much his senior in years; his second wife had borne him three children though sadly only one was living. He was locally known as Zik, a nickname borrowed from one of the politicians responsible for seeing Nigeria from colonialism into independence. The Ibuza Zik, who lived at Umuodafe, had the same proud carriage and charismatic bearing of the politician as a young man, and as he walked seemed to be forever scanning something in the clouds. His very long legs, which were always exposed on his way to the farm, or when he did his *aja* bit, ended up in a pair of the most pliable feet imaginable. He seldom wore shoes and as his heels never touched the ground he seemed to be perpetually dancing on the balls of his feet. He was very good at composing and singing the *aja* songs. And he was always laughing. He was simply that sort of rare specimen that seems unable to grow old.

Aku-nna liked Zik. He gave her solos to sing, and she was chosen to be one of the girls to sing the praise names of the age group — telling the story of their birth in song, how they had been given to the people of Ibuza to comfort them for the loss they suffered in the deaths of the other drowned girls. Aku-nna was to sing Zik's praise name and tell the audience in *aja* song

102

that, were it possible for relatives to intermarry, she would choose Zik. The other girls would join in the chorus, singing, "Ah . . . eee . . . !" in agreement.

The girls talked and dreamed about their outing dance. They worked and saved hard to buy their *jigida,* the red and black beads which they would wear above their bikini-like pants. Apart from these their tops would be bare, displaying the blue-coloured tattoos that went round their backs, then under their young breasts, and met at the heart. Their feet would also be bare, but small bells were to be tied round their ankles, so that when in the dance they jumped, or curtsied, or crawled in modesty, the bells would jingle in sympathy. It was to be the great moment of their lives and they knew it. In their old age, with clay pipes in their toothless mouths, they would turn to their grandchildren and say, "When we were young and our breasts were tight as tied ropes, we did the *aja* dance. It was the best dance in the whole land, and we did it."

In the afternoon of one Olie market day, about twelve of them decided to go for firewood. They had been to the stream that morning and had washed their clothes and bathed. Aku-nna had been claying the floor of her mother's hut, and welcomed the idea of a change. If she would have preferred to sit round and gossip with her friends, about their dance or about their men friends, she did not say, for she would rather follow the others than be left alone with her thoughts. She took her big cutlass and the ropes, and went with Obiajulu and Ogugua to fetch the rest. They felt safe and strong when there were many of them. They could tease old men on their way through their farms, they could sing, no enemy could terrify them; not that they had any enemies, but in Ibuza a young girl must be prepared for anything to happen. Some youth who had no money to pay for a bride might sneak out of the bush to cut a curl from a girl's head so that she would belong to him for life and never be able to return to her parents; because he had given her the everlasting haircut, he would be able to treat her as he liked, and no other man would ever touch her. It was to safeguard themselves against this that many girls cropped their hair very close; those who wanted long hair wore a headscarf most of the time. But when they were twelve strong, a man or boy who dared to attempt such a thing knew that he would be so mobbed that if he lived to go home to his mother

103

she would not even recognise him.

When they reached the abandoned farm where they were to find the firewood, they scattered into the bush, agreeing to give each other a cat-call to indicate that they were ready to leave. With each piece of wood you had to pull, then shake it, and if it still did not come free when you pulled again you used your cutlass. Aku-nna had been trying hard for a long time with one piece of icheku wood, which looked deceptively dry on the surface but just would not give way. At this rate she would have to leave it and look for some other wood, or she would never be ready by the time the others started calling for them to go home.

With all her power, she gave another final push, and the wood broke and crashed to the ground, sending her crashing along in its wake. At the same moment she felt the needle-like pain in the back of her waist. This would be the third time, and she knew now what to expect. She still had not told her mother, but this time is would be impossible to hide, for the others were bound to know. All this passed through her mind as she lay there on the dry twigs, looking at her hand that bled and knowing that she was losing equally between her legs. Her thoughts were in a turmoil of indecision about what to do next. Her closeness with Chike had crystallised and was now so established that she could not make a decision without wanting to know his opinion. But he was not here on this farm. He might be miles away from Ibuza for all she knew, judging by the distances he could cover with the new autocycle he had just bought. She came to the conclusion that there was no alternative open to her but to let her mother know. She sensed what this would mean; she would no longer be regarded as a child who knew nothing, but as a young woman on the verge of parenthood. It was not that she shrank from becoming an adult, but she was afraid of what her people might force the future to hold for her. If only things could go on being as they were now, with Chike seeing her every market day at Asaba, and the two of them sitting by the river bank in the quiet place they had discovered for themselves, doing nothing, just talking and talking, and he teaching her all the latest songs from a record song book he had ordered from Lagos. Once or twice he gave her a gentle caress but was careful to stop himself from going too far, for to him she was something apart, something pure that he did not want to pollute. She was beginning to know this and to respond to his unspoken wishes. She was beginning to realise too that though Chike might talk endlessly in the classroom, because it was his job, when he was by himself or with her he preferred silence. Sometimes they listened to the music of the river and the noises made by the leaves of the nearby bushes, but in the main they simply listened to their hearts.

That Chike was a man who for the first time in his life had fallen uncontrollably in love was plain to see. Over and over again his father had warned him that he was sticking his neck out dangerously, but Chike wanted it understood that he was not about to leave for any university without Aku-nna. He had politely told his father, who had been annoyed and began to bellow in his anger, to keep his money. He and Aku-nna would manage somehow. What was the point of getting a degree anyway? It might enhance his position but it would not necessarily make him a happier person. For several weeks his father had sulked and refused to talk to him, until Chike's mother went to plead with him, saying her son was becoming emotionally sick, not talking to her, not eating much and looking so unhappy that she was sure something was going wrong in his head. She begged her husband to talk to their son, to please instil in him that there were many fishes in the water, to remind him that he was only young and had a rosy future still in front of him.

Ofulue saw that his wife, Chike's mother, was a worried woman. He had been a teacher in a little town called Obankpa when he had married her, a frightened, thin woman with so much beauty and yet unaware of it. She had a way of remaining calm, of never raising her voice or shouting, even when bearing her children. She was his peace. Most of her children took after her. But if the boys were quiet like their mother, they were all sexually over-active and it could not be from her that they inherited this for she was demure as a nun, eyes always down and alluring in an understated way. Nor could it be from him; none of his four wives could complain that he ever over-taxed them sexually. But he had passed on to Chike all the maleness a man could want. And he loved his son because he had taken on from his mother all the beauty she had had to offer.

Ofulue made it up with Chike, who told him then that he intended leaving Ibuza to go and work with the new international oil company prospecting at Ughelli. He had chosen this town, only about a hundred miles away, because there many of his Urhobo classmates owned small mud houses with zinc roofs where he and Aku-nna might find a first home. They would have to elope; there was no other way. He could not be happy with any other woman and he was certain there was no man but himself in Aku-nna's mind.

His father pointed out that though Ibuza people would stick together in times of trouble, they would never forgive anyone who made the grade while they failed. He had existed among them knowing how far they were ready to bend, and not asking anything beyond that. Some considered this attitude too full of pride, because he had never given them cause to refuse him a favour. He had had to buy the land where he now grew cocoa beans, whereas other men would have just planted and afterwards claimed it as theirs. Ofulue's way suited him better for no one could then tamper with his property without inviting big legal trouble. What Chike was asking his father to do was to give the people a first opportunity to say "No" to him. Not only would they refuse but they would say, "No, you are an *oshu*."

Chike had been embarrassed by this frankness of his father's, so choked with emotion. He apologised for being such an impossible son, but what was he to do?

"I dream about the girl — I see her in everything, in the stream, I see her smile when I am riding alone, I hear her small voice when birds sing. I cannot tell you how happy we are when we have dumped her plantain into the Niger and can just sit and talk. . . ."

His father, who had been looking blankly at the wall opposite and smoking his pipe as if it were a pipe of peace, asked him to repeat what he had just said, and after hearing Chike's explanation he asked, now amused:

"So who pays for the plantain you dump into the river?"

"I do, Father. She can't carry much, so the whole bunch only costs three shillings — she buys them for a shilling and sixpence and is meant to sell them for three. I tell her to get the lightest and smallest bunch and I wait for her at Cable Point, then after we have dumped the plantain we have the whole day to ourselves. That's how we have come to get to know each other better. I wouldn't get to talk to her otherwise — there are always people in their hut, or her mother is there with her funny stories. So we had to devise this way, until she can also get teaching work after Christmas."

"There is one thing I beg of you. Whatever you do, don't spoil that girl — don't disvirgin her before you are sure she will be your wife. There is no worse fate for any woman in this town than that of one who arrives at her husband's couch polluted."

"No one is having her but me," Chike insisted.

"And you are not stealing her, either. We may be descended from an *osu* woman, but I like to do things in the proper manner. Tell me when she becomes a woman, then we shall go and speak to her people."

"But, Father, if they refuse, what are we going to do?"

"You are dancing yourself tired before the music has even begun. Wait until it starts. If the tune changes, we too will change with the tune. But we cannot do anything until the music starts. Keep your ear to the ground and be watchful, so that you will not be the second to ask for her when she becomes a woman. Be very careful."

There was no need for his father's cautioning. Chike knew already that he had to tread carefully. There was no escaping the fact that their ancestors had been bought. If they had been a poor and a nobody family, things might even have been easier; but they happened to be the Ofulues of Ibuza, and that was very painful for the people whose ancestors were Umejeis. What these people sometimes forgot was that Umejei too had come from somewhere else, from Isu, that he had not always lived there. In short, all the Ibuza people were immigrants; the *oshus* just happened to be new immigrants. It was a phenomenon of human societies found not only in backwoods places like the little towns of Ibuza, Asaba or Okpanam, but also among the very civilised peoples of America, Britain and Russia; it was in this that the Ofulue family, being well read, took consolation. As long as they did not expect any concessions from the people of Ibuza, as long as they kept their respectable distance, they could enjoy their wealth and elevated position in peace.

The last time Aku-nna and Chike had met, he had told her of some of this discussion with his father, mentioning the points he knew would put her mind at rest: that his father had said she

107

was a good girl, that he had known her father, that they should not go too far without a proper marriage. Although he skipped the nastier parts about the difficulties, she had been aware of them.

"Are your parents coming to ask for me in the proper way from my parents?"

He had nodded mutely and looked away, nervously twisting and retwisting her plaited hair until her head hurt. She did not ask any more questions, for she knew already that there would be trouble.

The sun was moving down from the middle of the sky to the east, and when it was time for them to part he held her tightly until he felt her heart beating very fast, and the nipples of her unconstrained breasts seemed to dig into his chest. They were standing in the shade of a big tree, the name of which their minds were too busy to recall, and he released her gently. Aku-nna sighed, near tears, and he himself was disturbed and was shaking, but he took her hand, stooped to pick up her plantain basket and led her out into the open. At Cable Point they parted, and he promised to come to their hut in a few days' time. She had said a wet goodbye.

It was this very evening that he was due to come, and now this was happening to Aku-nna on this farm before she had had time to see him to prepare for their next move. Her friends would certainly have to know about her condition when it came to crossing the stream on the way home. Would she have to be carried over it, or would the god or whoever owned the river be reasonable enough to forgive her crossing it even though she was unclean? After all, she had not known it was going to happen like this, on this farm, in this scorching heat. It was best to ask her friends' advice rather than to make a mistake and be condemned as an outcast leper for the rest of her life.

They must have missed her, for she could just make out a buzz of voices. Her cousin's sounded tearful, even at this distance, and quite agitated. They were still too far to hear her clearly if she shouted to them, so Aku-nna tried to get up and found that it was very painful, for she had actually knocked her back on the dry, hard earth, covered with sharp-edged weeds. Soon she recognised in the crackling noises of parched leaves the steps of someone approaching. The person obviously had a premonition that she was nearing where Aku-nna lay trapped in pain, for she called softly, as if in the presence of something holy.

"Aku. . . ."

"I'm here," she replied in a hoarse whisper. She was not badly hurt; what she lacked was the energy to confront the world of her people. The shock of being forced so suddenly to face up to this merged with the shock of her injury to such an extent that she could no longer tell which pain belonged to which, or which was worse. She thanked God now that the girl who had found her was her cousin Ogugua. She beckoned to her to sit down, and told her all.

Aku-nna was resigned to the fact that things would be different after that day, but she had not bargained for her cousin's instant reaction. Ogugua hugged her tightly with joy, laughing and telling her in her high voice that at last she was fully a woman. Before Aku-nna could stop her, she jumped up and screamed for the others to come — to bear witness that they had gone out to fetch firewood with a girl but that they would be returning home with a grown woman!

There were more crackling sounds around them and the others emerged, coal-black maidens with lightness in their step, like young goddesses let loose by a kind god. They were curious to find out what had kept Aku-nna down there among the twigs and dry cassava leaves; they were curious to know why it was that Ogugua was so excited. They came, their necks craned like those of young giraffes looking for fruits in the tops of trees, and Ogugua told them the good news. For to her it was that; they had been wondering and worrying if Aku-nna would ever become a woman, and now she was happy, and she was sure her family would also be happy. The girls' laughter was like the sound of clear bells on a Christmas morning. They danced and did a mock *aja* salute, then, no longer in a hurry to go home, they all sat down and asked her with gentle but dignified concern how she felt and whether she could walk home. She said she could, for had not their spirit affected her own? They stayed there for a while, chatting away and talking lightly and unconcernedly, like all young girls in the spring of their lives, planning their marriages, looking forward to their coming *aja* dance, laughing and giggling out of sheer happiness.

It was decided that the god of the river would forgive Aku-nna this time, for how was a girl to know when and where she would become a woman? It was agreed, however, that she should walk through the shallow waters as quickly as possible, and not linger to bathe; and the very next day Ma Blackie would have to come and sacrifice a day-old chick to the stream. The whole episode sounded so elaborate that Aku-nna felt mean, knowing that she had hidden her two previous periods. Because her bunch of dry wood was so light the others promised to compensate by giving her mother some of theirs.

The sun was going down and they knew that by then most farmers would already have gone home. The less people they met the better. However on their trek back to the stream, chattering and once or twice bursting into song as they went, they came across no one. Obiajulu asked Aku-nna if she had any idea whom she was going to marry, and Aku-nna said that she did not know.

"But many men have asked for her," Ogugua confirmed, "and my father told them she was still a child. Not after today, though."

"Do you know which families have asked for her?" another girl wanted to know.

"The Nwanze family of Umuidi and the Chigboes of Umuokpala. And one other family, from Umueze — I can't remember their name but, Aku-nna, you know their son. The fair-skinned one with a limp. He was in the same class as you at school, and he talks too much, or so I hear."

Aku-nna stopped short at this news. Then she exclaimed, "You mean Okoboshi? Yes, I know him. You say his father came for me for his son?"

"Yes, didn't you know that it was because of you they came most evenings?"

The others laughed and agreed that it was just as well for a girl not to know such things until she was fully grown, otherwise she might start being disobedient to her parents. And another thing, the price had to be settled; Aku-nna would fetch a big sum because she had attended school so long.

She felt like screaming at them to stop. She felt like boasting that, as far as she was concerned, it was Chike and nobody else — they must all know about the friendship between her and Chike. But friendship was one thing, marriage another. For a girl from a good family to marry the descendant of a slave would be an

110

abomination, *ife alu.* Little by little, the warm joy she had felt only minutes before seeped away. She thought of Chike, with the little beard he was trying to grow to frighten evil eyes away from her, of his gentle caresses and low, sad voice, of his eyes which mirrored all the worries in his mind. She had grown so used to him that she only had to search those eyes, deep set behind the glasses he sometimes wore, and without his saying a word she would know what she was to do. How could the world be so blind? Could not everyone see they belonged to each other? She had never felt so strongly about anything in her life. Imagine that foul-mouthed Okoboshi, who had never said a nice word to her, wanting to marry her! Her mother would never permit it. Anyway, she was going to teach for a year or two before thinking of marriage, her mother had agreed. Ma had told her, "I am not allowing you out of my sight until you are seventeen, or you are bound to die of childbirth. You are so thin and not very developed. All you have are legs and eyes." This consoled her. She was quite sure that her uncle, now her step-father, would consent and let her teach for a while to help her mother.

But Aku-nna did not realise many things. She did not know that her uncle wanted to be an Obi, how much he wanted the *Eze* title. She did not know that her mother Ma Blackie was expecting a child for Okonkwo and was at that early emotional stage of pregnancy when all she wanted was peace and to think of her unborn child, and was so deliriously happy that she would give in to anything rather than upset the man who was author of her present happiness.

The girls grew quiet as they reached the stream. Except for two middle-aged women further down who were mashing their cassava for the evening meal, the women's area was completely deserted. The men's side was a bit busier; boys on holiday liked to splash about there and fish, after being on the farms all day. A few of them were having a bath, and they were all joking and making fun of an old man who as usual was relating the story of his life.

"My first wife ran away," he was telling them, "because I beat her up. My second wife died when she was having a child. My third one had to go, because I fed her for seven entire years and she bore me no child."

"You should not have sent her away. She was a very good cook, very good at making crab soup. It was always delicious."

This last voice floated across to the girls on the other side of the stream, who were now faced with the dilemma of whether it would be all right for Aku-nna to cross with everyone watching, because by the time the evening meals had been eaten, people would know all that had happened on the farm. But relief had flooded over Aku-nna, for she had recognised the voice replying to the old man. It was Chike's younger brother Isito, home on vacation from the teacher training college at Ubiaja; she knew that the two brothers always moved together. The old man's stories were so preoccupying that at first the girls went unnoticed.

"Yes, she does cook well, but I also want a child. A male child as fat as a plump yam to inherit all my properties."

The boys all laughed at this, since everyone knew that Okolie had nothing but his grass-covered mud hut, his loin cloth and a pipe organ, which he only stopped playing to talk, eat or smoke his clay pipe.

It was old Okolie who saw them first. "Look at those beauties coming from the farm at this time of day! What have you been doing? Is anything the matter?" He bent down and poured a fistful of sand on his back, then walking forward, his naked dry body in full view of the girls, he said, "Rub this sand on my back, please. It has been a very hot day and my back is covered with prickly heat."

After a moment's hesitation, the girls greeted him with his praise name: "Bringer of peace."

In reply he said, "You shall have peace in your life, my girls." Still showing his back with the sand on it to Obiajulu, he repeated, "Rub the sand in, please. It has been a hot day."

"We will just go and stand our firewood at the other side, then I shall come back to rub the sand on your old back for you." Obiajulu's voice was too low to be normal.

People looked up from whatever they were doing. Even Chike, who was very far down on the quiet side of the stream thoughtfully fishing, turned in their direction. Aku-nna crossed quickly with her friends, praying that the god of the stream would be lenient with her for this terrible sin she was committing.

Obiajulu and the other girls discarded their knee-length lappas on top of the pile of firewood, covered their private parts with the beads they wore round their waists, and returned to wash away the mud from the farm in the stream. Aku-nna waited on the bank.

"Aku-nna, are you so shy that you cannot have your bath with your age-mates?" Okolie croaked like a frog with a bad cold. "What is the matter with you? Shy people are usually sly people as well. Look at me, I have nothing to hide. Why then should you with your young body be ashamed? When will you be proud of your body, if not now when you are approaching ripeness?"

He waded to where she stood with her arms across her chest in a modest attempt to cover her breasts. He peered at her, while almost everybody at the stream seemed to have been hypnotised by his voice, for they had all stopped what they were doing and simply stared at the two of them.

"I don't know what the world is coming to. When I was young, girls of your age never thought of clothes. It was only after marriage that women tied loin cloths, not before. Look at all your friends with heavy *jigida* beads around their waists just to cover their nakedness. . . ."

Other voices joined in and all started to talk at once. Chike had seen her, and, unsure that she had seen him yet, began to whistle their favourite tune, "Brown skin gal, stay home and min' baby". Her eyes followed the direction from where the song came, and she saw him, standing there, his fishing rod in his hand, his face turned away so that people would not suspect that it was for her that he whistled. She looked for just long enough to be certain that she was not imagining things — she had learned that if she stared people would guess what she was thinking — then sighed with relief, telling herself that all would be well since Chike was there at the Atakpo stream.

Suddenly she realised that Okolie was still talking and that the housewives mashing cassava on the other side were answering him back.

The louder of the two women told him, in language far from decent, that it had been his gabbing, gabbing all the time that drove his third wife Adaolie away. Why did he never mind his own business?

"I was only trying to help, to find out if she needed any help."

"Then wait until she asks you for it, bringer of trouble," rejoined another younger woman who with her equally young husband was just coming from their farm.

113

By now everyone had deduced what had happened. The middle-aged women whispered to each other conspiratorially. The young woman smiled knowingly to her husband, and the boys at the opposite end of the stream began deliberately to talk of other things in voices so loud that it was clear to all that they were trying to behave as if incidents of this nature occurred every day.

Chike packed his fishing gear, wound a colourful lappa round his swimming trunks, filled a little gourd he had with fresh water and gave a nod to his brother, indicating that it was time for them to go. Isito did not argue, for he saw a sort of troubled gleam in his elder brother's eyes, and he felt for him, as any friend would. He silently shared in his brother's unhappiness, and the two of them waded their way through the shallow water, well aware that pairs of eyes followed their progress. When they came to where Aku-nna stood, Isito gave a friendly nod and moved on, but Chike stopped. He stood there watching her unmoved, hearing no other sound, though his nerves bayed like hounds at the moon.

He saw her only as she was in that moment. Yes, she had grown a good deal this past year. Her clear skin shone with the fresh oil of youth. She was tall and straight, perhaps with a tendency to a slight stoop, though the cause was easy to find: her small breasts, filling out rapidly like bread being baked in a hot oven, were becoming too heavy for her narrow shoulders. Those brown eyes that had a way of reflecting everything around her now looked very frightened. She looked at him appealing, then quickly began to stare at the cracked ground, aware that they were now being shamelessly watched as they were surrounded by human silence. He showed no signs of being conscious of the scrutiny. Aku-nna had grown up and, but for the laws of their land, all he wanted to do was to take her away, running up the hills of Atakpo, away to where they would see no one for many, many years, to where they would be all by themselves like savages of old, he hunting for their food, she waiting at their abode to receive his love and to give him hers.

He realised that these were all fantasies of his anxious mind. The dream world in which he had momentarily immersed himself drifted away as he felt his brother's tap on his shoulder. His eyes still addressed Aku-nna with the intensity of demand which he was accustomed to use only when considering the mysterious movements of the fishes in Ibuza's little streams on hot, quiet days.

114

"People are staring at us, brother," Isito mumbled rather unnecessarily.

The brothers climbed the hills through the gentling night into the village. In a town like Ibuza, people did not need newspapers and radio as local media; such modern means of spreading information were alien to them and, what was more, were too slow, and you had to be able to read and write in order to follow them. The elderly, who made the decisions about the life of a girl like Aku-nna, could do without such literary knowledge. What was the point of bothering to learn the alphabet, of what use would it be to them? It would not tell them which was the best season for planting yams; it would not tell them what their fate with a particular woman might be. They had their own methods of knowing these things without the benefit of the ABC.

The news of the happenings on the farm had preceded the girls home, as had speculation that Chike Ofulue, the son of a slave, had looked at the daughter of a free-born Ibuza citizen with desirous eyes.

It was therefore with gladness and apprehension combined that Ma Blackie welcomed her daughter home. She fussed over Akunna incessantly, instructing her loudly in the dos and don'ts of womanhood in their culture. She must not go to the stream, she must not enter her step-father's house, nor the house of any *Eze* chief, until it was all over.

Okonkwo was also very pleased, and presented her with a hen that had been protesting violently in his clutch. He told Ma to kill the hen and make some hot Nsala soup for her daughter who had now grown into a woman. He stood there in the fading light, eyeing her as one would a precious statue, inwardly congratulating himself on his luck in having had the opportunity to marry her mother. Now the entire bride price would come to him. Had he not given Ma Blackie the child she had been craving for years? He knew women. In the frame of mind in which Ma Blackie now was, his word would be law. He was on the verge of going back to his own house to think about which of the suitors would pay most quickly and the highest sum when his mind went to Chike, and he called out to Aku-nna.

The sudden harshness that grazed his voice startled her. It was so without warning that it would have been difficult for an onlooker to credit that the silken, caressing tones of a minute before

115

came from the same man as this new authoritative, almost wicked voice.

"Aku-nna, Chike Ofulue is only a friend. You must remember that. Now that you have grown, that friendship must gradually die. But die it must!"

He walked away, leaving her standing there by the egbo trees, for he must not come near or touch her now when she was unclean. She listened to his footsteps crunching the leaves as he went, not once looking back to see how she was taking this new restriction, and it seemed to prove to her that these men, these elders, did have feelings for some of the women they married. Okonkwo must know how she was going to feel. His life could not have been entirely loveless; he must have cared for some woman once, and been loved and cared for in return, otherwise he would surely not have come himself to congratulate Aku-nna on becoming a woman. But the way he had spoken just now was the voice of authority, that authority which was a kind of legalised power. He was telling her, not in so many words, that she could never escape. She was trapped in the intricate web of Ibuza tradition. She must either obey or bring shame and destruction on her people.

But what of Chike? Thinking of him she felt a kind of heavy sadness that hung solidly in her chest so that she felt tempted to try to wrench it out. She turned to her mother's hut and saw that the hen that only a short while before had been alive had now been killed. Her brother had summoned his friends and they chattered together like monkeys as they plucked the feathers from the poor chicken that had had to die so mercilessly, just because she was a woman. She was not going to eat it, she told herself; not that this resolve would have needed much persuasion to be made, for she had noticed that on the first day of every period the little pains and heaviness about her caused her to lose her appetite.

Another thought that was going through her mind made Aku-nna afraid. She was beginning to feel that it was unjust that she was not to be allowed a say in her own life, and she was beginning to hate her mother for being so passive about it all. Fancy her mother advising her to forget Chike and do as she was told, because some other man would come, equally well educated, more handsome, and the son of a somebody. She had always shown Ma

116

Blackie the little presents Chike used to buy for her, and now Ma dismissed them, saying they were the price he naturally had to pay for befriending the daughter of a free-born person. It made Aku-nna's stomach turn, so much so that when she was called to partake of the hen killed specially for her she said point-blank no, she was not hungry. Ozubu, Okonkwo's second wife, who was there with all her children to share in the honorary hen, began to scold and tell her in a clamorous voice how ungrateful she was. She was reminded of the fact that many other girls became women and their families had no money to buy even a pigeon to mark it, and now here she had been given a whole big fowl and she was behaving as if she owned the world. Ezebona, the apple of Okonkwo's eye and his youngest wife, told Aku-nna to mind her ways, otherwise people might think that she was spoilt. She said this with a giggle, the giggle of a woman who was not only in love with her husband but was also sure of his affection for her. The others, Ozubu, Ma Blackie and their children, looked at her with so much hate that she was forced to assume a serious and concerned expression.

The party outside Ma Blackie's hut went on and on until the moon shone. Everybody in Okonkwo's family was excited and cheerful. Even his querulous first wife was contented with the leg of the chicken Ma Blackie had sent her, nicely wrapped in banana leaves. The children formed themselves into a circle and started to tell stories. Some young boys and girls could be heard calling to each other to come out for their moonlight games, and others screamed and laughed as they played hide and seek among the many stately egbo trees and coconut palms. The older boys, young men on the verge of marriage and settling down, put on their T-shirts, tied their long lappas round their waists and went in search of sweethearts to pass the evening with. Ma Blackie and her friends sat there, reminiscing about how it had been on the days they had become women.

By now Aku-nna knew that, pain or no pain, she was expected to get up and receive the young men who would definitely be coming to visit her, and for the first time in her life she found herself really making an effort to look presentable. She swallowed two of the tablets which Chike had made sure she bought the last time they had gone to Asaba together; they deadened the pain, and she trusted the effect would last the night. She had hardly had enough time to change into the Sunday lappa which her mother had told her to tie, before there was a loud greeting outside the door. She could hear the male voice of her first visitor. It was that boy Okoboshi. He asked if he could enter, and Aku-nna answered from inside the hut that he should do so, that she would be with him in a minute.

She debated within herself whether to wear a blouse or not, and finally decided to put one on, even though it was so hot. It was better to suffer the heat than to allow that foolish boy to stare at her breasts and maybe hurt her in his wild play. She chose a pink blouse. She had bought it herself and everybody had complimented her on it. She had only worn it occasionally since then, but tonight something told her that she should wear a blouse; after all, she had about four good ones, so why should she not wear one of them at home, rather than wait until she was married to start covering herself? She knew that if only they allowed her relationship with Chike to continue, she would keep her body hidden so that he alone could look at her if he wanted to. Her heart ached and tears began to well up in her eyes again, this time because it looked as if she was going to be trapped into a marriage that she was helpless to prevent. *God, please kill me instead,* she prayed, *rather than let this be happening to me.* Her mind ached for Chike, and so did her body. There was another set of greetings outside and she was glad, for although she knew it was not Chike it provided an excuse for her to avoid Okoboshi's brutal play.

She came out offered the young men some *nmimi* fruits. Soon two or three more men came, and it was then that she stopped caring. She had no way of telling which of them would win her uncle's approval. They each gave her little presents, which she was forced to accept. They eyed each other with vexation and suspicion, while she sat there, listening to but not taking in their empty boasts.

Why had Chike not come? Surely they could not prevent him from seeing her? After all, he would be only a visitor, just like all these youths. Would the gossiping women outside the door embarrass him away? Was that why they sat there, pretending to be talking about their lost innocence, when all they were actually doing was keeping her a prisoner? Surely they would still allow her to teach, surely her mother would allow that. She had not even heard her examination results yet — how could they let all her efforts go down the drain? Frustrated tears flowed now, and Aku-nna was thankful that her mother's palm-oil lamp was smoky and dim.

Azuka, the son of Nwanze of Umuidi, was watching her rather closely. He enquired if she had a headache but she denied it. The others stopped talking for a while, sensing that she was unhappy. They all knew about Chike, but if there was one thing an Ibuza man would do for another, it would be to save him from anything abominable. This girl was not exceptionally beautiful. In fact, but for her education, there was nothing extraordinarily attractive about her. What appealed to all of them, though they did not realise it then, was the gentle helplessness about her; she would sooner have died than hit her husband back with an *odo* handle if he beat her. She always spoke her mind only when necessary, not before. In their different ways, they all loved her in their hearts, and thought that her weeping for Chike was the result of an infatuation she would grow out of, even before the birth of her first child. For what sane person would ever consider sharing her life with a slave?

She could hear her mother greeting somebody else, telling them that she would soon have to send everyone away because she needed her sleep. The rather unnatural hush outside told her who her new visitor was. The other young suitors had also guessed, by the time Chike came in and greeted them. Only Azuka answered; the others continued talking as though nobody had addressed them at all.

Aku-nna sought and caught his eye in the dim light; he looked downcast.

She made way for him on the mat where she was sitting but before he had a chance to sit down, Okoboshi came forward, dragging one foot in the limp he had which was the result of a snake bite when he was a small boy.

"I would like to sit there," he said to Aku-nna.

She opened her mouth and closed it again. She saw Chike clenching and unclenching his fists, and her unthinking reaction was to rush up to him and hold him tight, begging him not to fight. She dreaded what the outcome might be, with all five of the others against him.

"Please, let them alone, please!" she cried loudly, as if her heart would burst open.

119

To the other boys it was like some sort of entertainment. They began to laugh, and their merriment increased in volume when Okoboshi said:

"Imagine the son of a free man not being able to sit where he wants, just because the Europeans have come to pollute our land. In the olden days, you would have been used to bury the son that girl will give me when I marry her."

The laughter that accompanied the latter remark was more subdued. How was Okoboshi so confident he would be the one to marry Aku-nna? If the others thought his claim rather arrogant they buried it in their hearts, for they were facing a common enemy, Chike the son of a slave.

Chigboe's son rose and pulled Aku-nna away from Chike, saying as he did so: "Stop crying. You can die from crying like that, you know."

Then he added, to her, "Sit where you like. Okoboshi was only joking."

She obeyed silently and sat in the remotest corner of the room, very near to the door leading to her mother's inner room. Chike refused to sit but stood by the front door, still troubled by the anger he was being forced to suppress.

Okoboshi wanted him completely out of the hut; he knew what he was going to do. Without warning, Okoboshi walked up to Aku-nna and seized her roughly at the back of her shoulder; he grabbed at both her breasts and started to squeeze and hurt her. All at once the self-control that Chike had been taught in years of staying with missionaries left him. He struck Okoboshi a full frontal blow. He added another, and another, waiting for the other rivals to come and fight him in defence of their friend, but he was surprised to see that nobody came forward.

Only Ma Blackie intervened, realising that whatever sport the boys were having with her daughter inside the hut, it was time to call a halt. For the cry she had heard enamanting from her daughter was not that of a girl having fun with her suitors but the cry of a girl in agony. When she saw Okoboshi sprawling on the mud floor, she covered her mouth to control an involuntary scream. A trickle of blood was escaping from his mouth and the others were looking on perplexed, uncertain what to do. She pulled Okoboshi to his feet, and addressed her verbal assault at Chike.

"If you want to prove yourself a strong man, why don't you do it outside and pick a man who does not have a limp?"

"Mother," Aku-nna begged, "please don't say anything. Okoboshi was hurting me, he was. . . . Mother, look at my new blouse! He has torn it, he was so rough. He was wicked — oh, Mother, please listen. . . ."

Ma Blackie waved aside her pleas. "You mean you have nice breasts and don't want men to touch? Girls like you tend to end up having babies in their father's houses, because they cannot endure open play, so they go to secret places and have themselves disvirgined. Is that the type of person you are turning out to be? I will kill you if you bring shame and dishonour on us. How can he hurt you with all these others watching? And yet you allow a common. . . ."

She did not finish her sentence for at that moment Ozubu came in to ask why Ma Blackie was raising her voice so — she should not shout so much, in her condition. Ozubu wanted to know what the matter was, and the story was related to her, this time spiced to flavour. The long and short of it was that Aku-nna would have no one near her but the son of a slave. Ma Blackie cried and cursed her fortune in being saddled with such a daughter. Had any of them ever come across such fortune as hers? She must go and make sacrifices to her *chi*, her personal god, to change her lot. Had they ever seen a girl like this daughter of hers who was wanted by so many good families but who preferred to choose a common . . .

Aku-nna concluded that if her mother was going mad there was a little saneness in her madness. She noticed that her mother had not been able to bring herself to use the word "slave"; her conscience would not let her. If anyone had tried to make their stay in Ibuza comfortable, it was Chike. All those beverages and cans of milk they had been drinking had not come out of her father's money. Her mother knew that it was Chike who had been buying them; she had not had to persuade her mother that it was all right to accept help from Chike, who had insisted that her daily diet, like that of most people living in that town, lacked proper nutritional content. Aku-nna could remember well how he had explained that she needed it the more since she had to burn a great deal of emotional energy for her examination. Her mother knew all that. The only part she had not known about was their plantain dumping in the River Niger. What puzzled Aku-nna most was that here now was this same mother of hers, standing up and telling these people that Chike was not going to be the man for her daughter.

The bitterness Aku-nna was feeling had gone beyond tears. She had heard it said often enough that one's mother was one's best friend, but she was beginning to doubt it. Had her mother encouraged her to accept Chike's friendship in order to just use him like a convenient tool, to ferry them through a difficult period of adjustment? Had she known all along, had she ever had any doubts that they would not be allowed to marry? Or did she really believe that customs had relaxed to such an extent that their people would not mind? Aku-nna again studied her mother, who was now crying dramatically, and wondered whether she was crying because of the disgrace of her family being associated with the son of a slave striking down the son of a free man, or because her daughter's first, perhaps only, love was being shattered and taken away from her. She knew that Ma Blackie liked Chike; she had seen them sit and talk for hours when he had come visiting as she was busily preparing the evening meal. Oh, what kind of savage custom was it that could be so heartless and make so many people unhappy?

Aku-nna did not know how it had happened, but the next thing she knew she was standing beside Chike. Their fingers were not touching but the closeness was enough to give her strength. Friends and neighbours poured out comfort to her mother, trying to assure her that she, Aku-nna, was simply infatuated; that she would change and think of her mother more as she grew older. Okonkwo's senior wife, who was Ogugua's mother, pointed out that this should have been Aku-nna's happiest day, and now this had happened. She begged Okoboshi to take the insult like a man.

"Suppose," she asked him, "in years to come, she becomes your wife, will you not always remember this day and laugh over it?" Then she told Ma Blackie to stop being stupid, for she too was beginning to doubt those tears, and reminded her of her condition, of the baby she was carrying.

This was another surprise to Aku-nna. So her mother was pregnant. She now realised that she would never be allowed to teach before being married away. Her bride price would be needed

122

very quickly to see her mother through her period of confinement. She knew that Ma Blackie would let Okonkwo have his way, now that he had made her dream of being a mother once more come true. It was surprising that her uncle Okonkwo had not shown his face here throughout all the fighting and arguments, Aku-nna thought, but she discovered later that the reason was that he found undignified the prospect of coming out to quarrel with a slave's son, just because one of his stupid wives had allowed him into her hut.

The young men had to depart, as the night wore on. Nothing untoward occurred in the days following. They were such normal and restful days that sometimes Aku-nna wondered if she had imagined the hullaballoo of the night she officially became a woman.

The fifth night was hot and moonless. Aku-nna's period was over. She felt happy and free, especially after a good all-over bath at the stream, for she had been forbidden to go there before or to go to Asaba. For the past four days she had had to be content with half a pail of water daily, which was supposed to suffice; but it was never enough. There were so many soiled things of hers she would have liked to wash but she felt constrained, so she arrived at a compromise with herself, that she would wait and wash them all on the first day she was allowed to go to the stream.

It was with a sense of lightness and cleanliness that she answered Obiajulu's cat-call for them to go out to their dance practice, for her friends and age-mates knew that she would now be allowed into the dance hut. They took a paraffin lamp with them, one of Chike's presents (otherwise they would have used a piece of burning wood), and on their way they were joined by Ogugua and Obiageli. Just as they reached the sandy square called *otinpu*, meaning "a crying place", they saw another paraffin lamp coming towards them. It was Chike, and he recognised them first.

Without any reservation, they all greeted him. He touched Aku-nna's cheek and remarked that she looked happy.

"I have some good news for you, but I'm not really supposed to disclose it until tomorrow. I don't think it would be wise for me to tell you now, or your mind would not be on the dance and that would annoy your dancing instructor Zik."

The girls' voices begged him to please tell them. They promised to concentrate on the dance. If the news was a secret, they would tell no one. So please would he tell them.

Chike looked helpless in the midst of their pleas. As for Aku-nna — he could feel her heart beating fast. She had stopped bubbling like her friends, and her eyes were busy probing his, a feat she would not have accomplished had it been daylight.

"All right, let me be and I shall tell you everything," he said, freeing himself from the laughing girls. "It is simply this: your friend Aku-nna has succeeded in her examination. She can now be a teacher if she wants to."

This was greeted with shouts of delight. Obiajulu said she had been certain Aku-nna was going to be a success; she had seen it in a dream, she declared. They did not contradict her, for had not the dream come true? Had Aku-nna not passed the examination? They began to question Chike about the fates of the boys they knew. It was then disclosed that Okoboshi had failed.

"It serves him right. He never studied, only went about being spoiled by his mother, just because he has a slight limp."

"Don't say things like that," Obiageli admonished judiciously, for Okoboshi's mother and her mother were from the same household at Ogbewele. "You sound like an old witch full of revenge. He is the eldest of the whole family, the only son his mother has. His parents are bound to spoil him. He is not a bad boy really."

The other girls had to agree that there was nothing very bad about Okoboshi, only that he had been brought up to think the whole world belonged to him by right.

"I must go now," Chike said. "I can hear the voice of Ngozi, your soloist. The dance has started already." He touched Aku-nna again on the cheek, smiled and said: "Well done. I shall see you tomorrow and then talk over the teaching plan with your mother."

He waved them a final goodbye as he disappeared into the thick black night, his lamp making a bright halo, like the light of the three wise men of old. One or two of the girls sighed; Chike was one of those men whom women would always feel like cherishing and protecting, whether they turned out to be murderers, smugglers, or even the sons of slaves.

They started up their chattering again, this time more joyously, though they knew where to stop. Obiageli, Obiajulu, Ogugua and the rest could talk about their marriage plans. Obiajulu's bride price had already been paid; the chief who was marrying her had only had to pay the minimum twenty-five pounds because, as she bragged, her family was well off. Her father, who was also a chief, had not even wanted the money but had had to accept it as a token, otherwise her future husband might take her for granted.

"For my father does not want to be a god," she exclaimed, "he is perfectly satisfied as a chief. He has built a house with a zinc roof. He has good huts for all his wives. He does not need to ask for a great deal of money for his daughters."

The girls knew this to be true. Obiajulu's father, though he had six wives and a courtyard bursting with children, was so good at farming that he had earned himself the title of "Diji", meaning a good yam farmer. The trouble with that family, though, was that the girls were not celebrated beauties, because their father was such a very short man, and yet their tongues were very sharp. Many a husband of one of these Diji girls, too frightened to beat his shrew of a wife, would send her back to her father. The word was that they boasted of their father's achievements to such an extent that the new husbands found themselves inadequate. Ma Blackie had warned Aku-nna about this, instilling in her that no woman should carry her father's glories to her husband's house. As soon as a good woman was married, she must learn to exult in her husband's accomplishments, however small they might seem in comparison with her father's.

They were late for the dance, and Zik was not in the best of moods. He quickly ordered them to tie the little bells round their ankles, and told Aku-nna to change her lappa with the fish pattern for the short raffia skirt she was meant to wear for the dance. She left on her nylon blouse, because she had not yet bought the beads to wear across her chest. The others took their places, and Aku-nna found that she had to go through the salutation part several times before she got it right. She was so excited about her results, and so were her friends though they could not tell Zik of the good news yet, since he was still a bit angry with them for having kept him waiting. His mood did not improve with the blunders the girls were making in their parts.

"One would think you've all sold your legs, or that rats have been licking them in the night, the way you land so ungraciously like old women. When you land on the ground, do so with your toes. They won't break!" he cried, lashing his dancing whip about in search of an offender.

Aku-nna managed one of her songs, and landed so lightly and

125

gracefully that at last Zik rewarded them with his winning smile. Aku-nna was still poised on her toes, breathing quickly, her eyes flashing with pleasure at Zik's praise, when the oil lamps that illuminated the room were all knocked down by some force.

Heavy footsteps thudded into the hut, and there were strange voices, men's voices, suffused with an ominous sense of urgency. The sudden darkness and the irregularity of the whole situation stunned the girls into puzzled and shocked silence. Then, as abruptly as the silence had descended, all the girls began to shout and scream, from one end of the hut to the other. The screams intensified when one or two of them who tried to make for the door realised that it was being held closed by a powerful hand. There were thuddings of more feet, wrestling and jostling and while Aku-nna was trying to find her way in the confusion a muscular pair of arms grabbed her by the waist.

"Here she is!" she heard a voice announce. "Let us go!"

She could not scream, for her mouth was covered by a rough farmer's hand. It was obviously the hand of a practised kidnapper for he left her nose free to breathe. Her thoughts were wild. The pandemonium around her continued as her bearers made for the door. She could hear shrieking girls running out of the hut, and one or two of them who had probably collided with something in the pitch blackness were making miaou sounds like injured cats. She could hear Zik's voice, thundering and raging like a mad bull as she was being fast borne away on the shoulders of unknown, hefty men, who trotted like horses with wings for feet.

What was a girl to do in a predicament of this sort? There was no use in struggling. There must be at least twelve of these men, all running, running and breathing hard. So this was to be the end of her dreams. After everything, she was nothing but a common native girl kidnapped into being a bride.

The realisation was so painful, and the men carrying her moved so rapidly, swinging her from one shoulder to another, that a kind of dizziness overcame Aku-nna. Nature has a way of defending her own: when a pain becomes too much to bear, you lose consciousness. This was what happened to her. When she arrived at her new home in Umueze. Aku-nna was a limp bride in need of revival.

126

9

Escape

There was no need for Chike to hurry home, now he had given Aku-nna the good news of her success. He chuckled to himself at the surprise that had been written all over her face when he told her. He was relieved and very happy for her. At least it would make things easier for them both. He must see to it that she got the teaching post she so wanted; that would be a help to her people. There would be no reason to pressurise her into marriage at six-teen. It would give him time, too, to make up his mind between joining the oil company at Ughelli or going to the University at Ibadan, as his father had suggested. His father had also pro-mised to talk to Okonkwo about Aku-nna, though he was taking his time. Perhaps he was waiting for this result as well; and, knowing him, Chike suspected that one of his father's reasons for being so lukewarm about it all was that he considered Aku-nna too young, both in age and education. If only Okonkwo would agree, if only he would think of the girl's good rather than his per-sonal pride, the Ofulue family would willingly pay one full bag of money for her bride price — a bag of money was only the equivalent of a hundred pounds sterling, which to his family was no money at all. He must hurry and tell his father the news.

What a bad night, Chike observed. On nights like this, one could almost believe that God was a human, and tonight He was sad — gloomy and morose, judging from the dark sky. There were no shadows at all, and the thick trees seemed to be crowd-ing towards him with some evil doom. It was on nights like these that people were killed, bitten by snakes frightened into self-defence by the thickness of the dark. He stopped suddenly. He felt that somebody somewhere was calling out his name; but when he lifted his lamp, he saw nothing but the evil-looking trees with their thickset branches. He shuddered and would have run, but the call came again. This time the voice was clear: it was Aku-nna's. But that could not be; it was not long since he had left her with her friends on their way to practise in their dance hut. No, it was his mind playing funny tricks on him. Had not his mother often warned him never to take this short cut to Aku-nna's village, because this very bush was the place where those who had committed abominable sins were thrown? This was how the area earned its name of "bad bush". He walked faster, and his heartbeats also raced, for what reason he did not know.

Then he heard the firing of a gun. It was followed by another, and another and another. That was strange, he thought. He knew of no one in their village who was ill or dying. He thought hard, feeling concerned. Maybe a death had taken place abroad and the family had just been informed of it.

The firing had stopped, and he was now nearing his home. He could hear a faint bridal tune floating over from the other side of the village, and he had to laugh. What sort of a girl would choose a night like this — moonless, gloomy and formidable — to go to her husband's house? The funniest part about it was that he had heard nothing about it beforehand, though this might be explained by the fact that he had been away all day in Onitsha at a headmasters' meeting to discuss the examination results. He had been rather impatient with his sisters when he returned and perhaps that had put them off telling him about this unusual bridal night; no doubt Nneka, his youngest sister, would tell him about it in the morning.

He went straight to his father's house to break the news that Aku-nna had passed her examination. His father was glad, and told him that he had already begun talks with Okonkwo.

"You mean he did not say no?" Chike asked, incredulous.

His father smiled. "He did not say no and he did not say yes. Have you ever seen a person who was given some delicious fish and just puts it in his mouth?"

"No, Father, the person would have to eat it."

"Okonkwo will have to be bought. He wants to go to Udo to take the Eze title, and that would cost him more than he can produce from his farm in five years. We shall have to provide that money. But that will mean your marrying early, and I don't like it, not very much."

"But, Father, she is not sixteen yet. She can wait for me. She can take a higher course in teaching, or I can work with the oil company in Ughelli — I don't mind which of these plans you approve. All I want is that she should leave that family. She is being exposed to all kinds of insults."

"So I heard. And that you went so far as to knock that cripple down."

"Oh, he is not a cripple. He was extremely annoying and insulting. I just had to stop him."

During the pause in the conversation that followed, there were more gunshots and the sounds of songs and dances reached their ears. There was no doubt about it; someone very near them, on just the other side of Umueze, was getting married. His father put their thoughts into words.

"Who would be marrying a girl on a night like this? And from the way they are firing their guns one would think the bride was kidnapped."

Chike stared at his father but his image would not focus. His father looked like a man drowning in a big river — now you see him, now you don't. Chike did not know what was happening to him. Was he going to faint? Surely his father was still standing there in front of him, looking at him, talking to him; but all he could make out was this outline of a big, black man that kept coming and going. He held on to one of their leather armchairs for support. He heard himself asking his father, in a voice so alien, so hoarse that he could have sworn it was not from his own throat:

"Did you say the bride might have been kidnapped?"

Understanding dawned on the older man. So that was what Chike was thinking, why he was looking so strange. He could not answer his son in words. He shook his head, as though his tongue had been cut from the roof of his mouth as had happened to the slaves of old.

Chike padded slowly towards the door, like a duck carrying a ruptured egg. "I think the singing and gunfire came from the Obidis'." He paused, his eyes following the line on his father's floor as if he had never seen the greenish patterns there before. "I think they have kidnapped the girl I am going to marry, Father. That is what is making me feel sick."

Ofulue moved forward and laid a strong hand, damp from emotional sweat, on his son's shoulder. Chike whirled round and

129

wept unashamedly into his father's chest. Every tear seemed to hit the older man like the sharp end of a hot needle.

Ogugua, Obiajulu and many of the girls ran screaming, tearing home in terror. Parents were startled to hear their story. Some men had covered their faces, as men did during the yam festival masquerade, and broken into their dance hut. Nobody had known what was happening, but all of a sudden the lights had gone out — and it had been so dark you could not even see yourself. And they had all run home as soon as the hut door was thrown open again, because previously someone had closed it. Yes, that was strange, too; they always kept the dance hut door open, but they were sure someone had deliberately shut it. No, they were not hurt, though the men had thrown them into confusion.

Everyone wondered what it all meant. Ogugua's mother was sure the men were from a rival group who did not want the girls to perform their outing dance. Obiajulu was doubtful about this, for the men who handled her during the turmoil had searched her over as though they were looking for someone in particular, and she had been flung aside as soon as it was discovered she was not the person they wanted. She described this to her mother, while Ngbeke, Okonkwo's senior wife, was listening, and her mother slapped her mouth shut, telling her that a good woman did not repeat everything she experienced.

"You had better watch your tongue, the way you go parrotting on. Have you forgotten that you are betrothed to an important chief? You have to learn to keep your mouth shut. You are all safe, and well, so let these mysterious men look for their finds somewhere else."

The older women pushed the episode at the dance hut to one side, knowing that their menfolk would look into it. Zik was certainly not a man to take such an affront lying down. It was then that Ogugua told them about Aku-nna's success and the women momentarily forgetting their petty jealousies, shouted for joy. They were so thrilled that with one accord they decided to go and congratulate Ma Blackie and Okonkwo.

Ngbeke brought a burning piece of wood which she thrust to and fro to light their path to Ma Blackie's hut. It was not far, only a few yards away, but the night was so dark and their nerves were shaken by the dance disturbance. They did not want to talk about it much, for the more such an incident was talked about, the more it would be seasoned by exaggeration and the more frightened the girls would become. It was a happy bunch of people that went to Ma Blackie's house, to share her good fortune.

They were a little surprised that Ma Blackie had already gone to sleep. Ngbeke jokingly called her a lazy woman, retiring to bed so early. She warned her playfully that Okonkwo expected every wife of his to bear him strong and healthy sons, not sluggish ones who would go to sleep soon after the evening meal.

"It has been a tiring day for me," Ma Blackie excused herself. "I feel so weak, one would think I had never had a child before. It makes me so ashamed of myself. Please come in. I shall light the lamp. My daughter is still at the dance, and that lazy boy of mine never comes home unless he is tired, but do come in. . . ."

"Where did you say Aku-nna is?" Ngbeke asked. Her voice was so sharp that Ma Blackie's hand shook as she lit the palm-oil lamp.

"She went to the dance." Then she saw Ogugua and Obiajulu standing by the door. "Did you not go too? I thought you all came for her."

Ngbeke did not wait for any more talk. She shouted for their husband.

"Okonkwo-oooo! Okonkwo-ooooo. . . . Wake up, leave Ezebona alone. They have kidnapped our daughter. Wake up, wherever you are! Oh, my God! Wake up, all Ibuza, wake up all the dead both in heaven and in hell. An insult has been heaped upon us. . . ." She stopped for breath, and ordered the girls to fetch her the family gong.

The gong, shaped like a bell, when hit on the back with some metal object produced a loud and penetrating sound designed to hold people's attention. As the chief wife of the family, and the oldest woman, it was Ngbeke's duty to do this, to inform the whole of Ibuza of what had happened to them on this fearful night. She had already attracted many families with her announcements unaided by the gong, but with its arrival she could make herself heard in the nearby village of Ogboli. Ngbeke removed the top of her lappa and placed it on her head, a sign that she was in sorrow, and so she was. On occasions like this the women usually came together to cry their woes.

131

Now they were all crying, knowing that Aku-nna had passed her examination, remembering now what a kind, quiet girl she was. Okonkwo started to blame himself for allowing her to join in the dance of her age group in the first place, seeing that she was such a refined and intelligent girl. Iloba and all Okonkwo's other sons swore they would kidnap and cut locks of hair from the heads of all the girls in the family that was responsible for this outrage against their half-sister.

"One would have believed that we were all civilised now, and that this kind of thing had stopped happening," Iloba said thoughtfully.

As for Ma Blackie, she just sat there on the mud couch where a kind somebody had pushed her. The energy had been completely drained from her. Her daughter, for whom she had sacrificed so much for her education, kidnapped? A girl who did not know even half of the customs of Ibuza, kidnapped? Her mind could not register it.

Nna-nndo, who had been crying as much as anyone, stopped and followed the big boys in their search for the village, the family that had done this. The women, led by Ngbeke with the gong, went round the town crying:

"Who has stolen our daughter? Let him inform us!" Gong, gong, gong, gong. . . .

Even as they were doing all this, they knew it was useless. Aku-nna had gone. All the man responsible had to do was cut a curl of her hair — "isi nmo" — and she would belong to him for life. Or he could force her into sleeping with him, and if she refused his people would assist him by holding her down until she was dis-virgined. And when that had been done, no other person would want to take her anymore. It was a shame they had not known or guessed in time what was happening; they might have been able to save her, so her people thought. But whatever family was keeping Aku-nna was taking its time about officially informing them; it must be that they planned to make sure she could not be taken back, before announcing where she was.

Ngbeke shouted until she was hoarse. Okonkwo ranted and fumed until he decided to console himself with his bottle of Ogogolo, a kind of native gin. It was the middle of the night, when the whole town was at last asleep, that three male members of the Obidi family came to disclose to Okonkwo that his step-daughter Aku-nna was lying peaceably on the mud couch specially prepared for her and her husband, Okoboshi.

There was nothing Okonkwo could do. They brought more gin to dull his senses, and a minimal amount was agreed upon as the bride price for Aku-nna. After all, she was just like any other girl. All this modern education did nothing good for any woman; to say the very least, it made her too proud. More drink flowed, and Okonkwo prayed amid the pieces of kolanut scattered on the floor that Aku-nna would bear them many children. By the morning, when it was fixed they should meet again, they would have discovered whether Aku-nna was a decent girl or one of those who went to her husband's couch on their marriage night empty. Okonkwo assured them that his daughter was as intact as a closed flower. Nobody had touched her. The keg of palm wine they must bring must be of the very best kind, and it must be full and bubbling to its brim.

They parted as reasonably happy in-laws, whilst the women slept. Ma Blackie and her young son had very little rest. Nna-nndo had found out where Aku-nna was being held, for during all the confusion he had run to the only friend he knew he could trust not to harm his sister. He went to Chike, and between them they traced the singing and dancing to Okoboshi's family. Chike had vowed that he would get her back. But Ma Blackie and Nna-nndo wondered how.

Aku-nna arrived at her new home limp, half-conscious and half-clothed. The women there took her in, praising the smoothness of her body. She had not a single scar, and her hands were so soft. They giggled as the senior Obidi poured chalk, the symbol of fertility, on her breasts and prayed to his ancestors that Aku-nna would use it to feed the many children she was going to have for his son Okoboshi. They fanned her and blew into her ears, but she remained weak and listless, so somebody suggested the local gin. It burned Aku-nna's throat so that she coughed, and her new nurses laughed and welcomed her to her husband's home.

Okoboshi's mother came forward to talk to her, addressing her as daughter. She was a very plump woman, fair-skinned like her only son Okoboshi, for whom nothing was too much or too good. She was still beautiful in a placid, contented kind of way. Her voice was low and she lacked the nervous excitability the women in Aku-nna's family had. In fact all the females in this family seemed contented. They were not very rich but there was a certain smugness in the air that spelt communal satisfaction. She stared at the mouth of the woman who was now talking to her.

"You are not to worry. We shall send a message to your mother. You are in good hands. My husband decided to get you for our boy this way because we saw and heard of the part that slave boy wanted to play in your life. No girl from a family as good as yours would dream of marrying a slave."

"Oh, no," chorused the other women, shaking their heads. "It is never done."

They went on welcoming her and praying that she gave them many sons and daughters. One of the women, very young and with all the features of Okoboshi's mother with the difference that she was thin, introduced herself as Aku-nna's sister-in-law. She was married and had two babies but had come to the family home that afternoon in preparation for Aku-nna's arrival. She assured Aku-nna that marriage was a pleasant and relaxing way of life for a girl, especially if the husband was surrounded by relatives as Okoboshi was. She should not look so scared, for there was not going to be any pain, anywhere. It would be happiness all the way. In a few months' time, when she had conceived her first child, she would remember all she had been told tonight. The young woman showed Aku-nna a pile of new lappas which they had brought for her to wear; in fact they had already tied one round her waist to cover her short dance raffia skirt. And she smiled. They smiled a lot in this family, Aku-nna noticed.

They took her into a room where the mud couch had been colourfully painted, and on the other side was a wooden bed, spread with a white *otuogwo* cloth that was edged with red checked patterns. On the centre of the bed was a white towel, foreign-made, judging from its softness. That was to be one of the presents her mother would receive in the morning, stained with the blood she was going to shed on being disvirgined. Aku-nna scanned it all and shuddered. The others laughed at the grimace on her face, and again assured her that it would not be painful and that Okoboshi had been particularly instructed to be gentle with her.

"You never know," the sister-in-law confided with an air of feminine know-how, "you may even like it the very first time."

Again they were all laughing, so pleased with their new bride. But the bride herself could not smile, nor talk, nor even look them in their faces for long.

This caused another young woman, a relative of course, to ask, "Maybe you don't like us?" and this girl was hustled out sharply, chided by the low voice that reminded Aku-nna very much of Okoboshi.

"No girl likes to be kidnapped. Go out and join in the dancing."

Soon afterwards, most of them left, but many people still came in to see the new wife, to greet her and offer prayers for her. The men outside went on drinking and firing guns for so long that Aku-nna became stiff from sitting listening on the mud couch. As for that bed, only her corpse would ever lie there, she told herself.

Okoboshi's sister brought her some water and asked if she would like to wash. She shook her head; but she would, however, like to be shown where their women's toilet was. Her new sister-in-law agreed to show her, warning her that she must try not to be difficult, because Okoboshi would only have to call for help and all those drunken men would come in and help him hold her legs apart so that he could enter her with no further trouble. The men would not be blamed at all, because it was their custom and also because Okoboshi had a bad foot.

Aku-nna was listening very hard, but her mind was too numb to react to everything the woman said. All she knew was that if that should happen, she was not leaving that house alive in the morning. She was determined that she would kill herself in the night. How she would do it, she did not know. But she was not going to be a willing bed-partner to somebody she did not love and who had never spoken a single kind word to her in her whole life.

Then she heard the whistle. Her numbed mind came alive. It was the one and only song with which Chike always called her, it was their message and their love song. It could be nobody but Chike.

"Brown skin gal, stay home and min' baby,
Brown skin gal, stay home and min' baby,
I'm going away in a sailing boat
And if I don't come back stay home and min' baby. . . ."

Her first impulse was to run in the direction of the whistle; but even as the thought came to her, she realised that it would

135

have been an empty attempt. She must take her time, she must think out the best way. Okoboshi's sister stood there by the gate leading to the *owele*, watching her. The noise of the dances and the music and merrymaking of the men in the Obidi compound was still to be heard, but the only living sound that Aku-nna's ears acknowledged was that whistle. The wild, joyous outbursts of the celebrators to her might as well be the cries of ghosts burning in hell, though they could be dangerous if she tried any escape now. There was a comforting feeling of security in her knowledge that she was also being watched by Chike, and that moment clinched her determination. If ever she got out of this alive, there was no man for her but Chike, slave or no slave.

She was taken back to the hut, a prisoner being led by a warder. Just once she turned her head towards the whistling and waved a goodbye to the air, not bothering to wonder what anyone might make of it, as she walked quietly back to the room. Inside she flopped down on the mud couch and faced the wall, shutting her eyes very tightly. Her new sister-in-law was doing more talking, trying to soothe her, but Aku-nna made no response.

She must have slept, for when she opened her eyes in the dim light it was with the realisation that a pair of eyes were scanning her very being. Uneasy, she sat up, and unbidden the happenings of the past hours flooded back to her. Anger and despair descended on her, and her mouth tasted the bitterness of it. Then it was that she looked up at the man standing in front of her, and saw that it was Okoboshi. He was in the process of wrapping round himself a big lappa with shell patterns on it, which Aku-nna had never seen him wear before. It was so voluminous and so cleverly tied about his thin waist that it hid his disfigured foot. In fact he looked quite well-to-do and handsome standing there, admiring her with amusement. He was smiling, just as his mother did, though his version of that smile had a kind of crookedness about it; instead of gracing the centre of his face, the smile was drawn lop-sidedly towards one of his ears. It was the smile of an embittered young man. Okoboshi was going to be wicked. He was going to be difficult. He hated her, that much she could see.

A kind of strength came to her, from where she did not know. She knew only that, for once in her life, she intended to stand up for herself, to fight for herself, for her honour. This was going to be the deciding moment of her existence. Not her mother, not her

136

relatives, not even Chike, could help her now. She waited, planning that, if the worst came to the worst and she had to fight physically, she would go for his weak foot. Her glance moved down the flowing lappa as she tried to guess which was the sensitive limb, the effect of Okoboshi's childhood wound, which had healed badly and left a ghastly pink scar that ran from knee to ankle, had been to make one leg shorter than the other. But when he stood still, as he did now, it was impossible to tell that he had a limp. He followed her gaze and seemed to be reading her thoughts, for his smile broadened almost to include the entire room which had been so artistically set by adoring relatives for the enjoyment of the groom.

"I am sorry you do not like me. Why is that? Is it because I have a limp? Our child will not limp, he will be perfect. So what is the trouble? You should be glad," he said still smiling sinisterly, still standing like a statue. He had left the top of his body bare, for the moonless night was very hot and the fact that they were enclosed in this small room with very tiny windows did not at all improve the temperature.

What a smooth skin he had, Aku-nna thought absently. As for a suitable reply to give him, she did not know where or how to begin. She sat there bolt upright, staring demurely at the shell patterns on his big lappa, but ready to spring. He moved closer, and her head shot up like that of a wary cobra.

Okoboshi laughed outright at this, but his laughter was too loud to be true. She thought she detected a panicky ring in that laughter, though she was far from sure; but it was certainly a hollow laugh, the laugh of an unsure man. He limped away and sat on the wooden bed, making it give out a whining noise that sounded creepy in the middle of this night. Aku-nna sighed; he was not going to use force, thank God for that.

But she was wrong. The very next minute he was upon her, pulling her roughly by the arm, twisting the arm so much that she screamed out in pain. He forced her onto the bed, still holding on to her arm, which she felt going numb. She recalled then that Okoboshi was a very good wrestler who liked to take his opponents by surprise; the reason Chike had been able to floor him that night was simply that Okoboshi himself was unprepared. But tonight he was ready for Aku-nna. When she kicked him in the chest, he slapped her very hard, and she could smell the gin

137

on his breath. She knew she could not overpower him. The slap had been painful and she was bleeding inside her mouth. Tears of desolation flowed from her eyes as he knelt over her, untying his lappa with shaky hands. His chest was heaving up and down like a disturbed sea. If she was hoping for mercy and understanding, she was not going to get it from this man. He was too bitter.

Then she laughed, like a mad woman. Maybe she was mad, because when later she remembered all that she said to Okoboshi on that bed she knew that the line dividing sanity and madness in her was very thin. Out came the words, low, crude words, very hurtful and damaging even to herself.

"Look at you," she sneered, laughing mockingly all the time. "Look at you, and shame on you. Okoboshi the son of Obidi! You say your father is a chief — dog chief, that is what he is, if the best he can manage to steal for his son is a girl who has been taught what men taste like by a slave."

Okoboshi stopped short in mid movement, his shakiness ebbing away, relaxing the knees he had planted on her arms. Yes, she saw the effects of her words and she continued, talking and laughing hysterically, her eyes never leaving his face.

"Yes, he has slept with me, many, many times. Do you want me to tell you when it started? I'll tell you. That afternoon at school, that day when you and your friends made me cry. Yes, that was the day. If you remember, I did not come back to the class. I went home, because it was too painful for me to sit on the hard bench. Yes, have you heard our results? I passed. And you failed," she taunted. "So even if you take me now, that white towel of your mother's is never going to be blessed by any blood from me. I have already shed it to make another very good man happy."

Okoboshi was now standing up on the floor. His mouth was wide open, his eyes stared at her, as if the snake that had bitten him years ago was now lying on that bed poised to bite into his very being again.

Aku-nna did not let up, but persisted, warming to her subject. "Even if you do sleep with me tonight, how are you ever going to be sure that the child I might bear would be your own? I may already be expecting his child, and then you would have to father a slave child. What a come-down for the great and mighty Obidi family! For I should never stop telling my son whose child he was."

138

"But you were unclean until two days ago. My mother said so," Okoboshi half-heartedly protested, his voice sounding distant.

"Oh, yes, that is true. But today I passed my examination. We celebrated my success together," she snarled, her heart thumping in the knowledge that his people had probably been watching her all that day. She hoped Okoboshi would not ask any more questions, or else he might discover that she was making it all up. He had one more query.

"Where did you celebrate your success today?"

"In his house, of course. I go there often."

That was the last straw. Luckily he did not ask her to describe Chike's house, but what he did do was to condemn her, to curse her. He would never in this world touch her. She had brought shame on all the people who had been unfortunate enough to come into contact with her. She was nothing but a common slut, fit to be kicked around and spat upon by slaves, because in her last incarnation she had been a slave water-carrier, only good enough to be given to gorillas for them to sleep with. She was not a human being, but a curse to all human beings. He filled his mouth with soapy saliva and spat, *plop,* in her face between her nose and her mouth. The slimy spit revolted her and she almost vomited, but she was determined to suffer it through.

"If you really want to know," Okoboshi concluded, "I was not too keen on you anyway. My father wanted you simply to get even with his old enemy Ofulue, your slave lover's father. So you are not a virgin! That will be the greatest fun of it all. You will remain my wife in name, but in a few months I shall marry the girl of my choice and you will have to fetch and carry for her and for my subsequent wives. Get out of my bed, you public bitch!"

With this, he hit her so forcefully in the eye that she was sent reeling onto the mud couch.

She did not know for how long she lay there unconscious, but she was awakened by the crow of a lonely cock. When she tried to rise from the couch, her feet gave way and she fell again; so stiff and painful was her body that morning. Okoboshi was still sleeping the sleep of the just bridegroom who had been tricked into marrying a girl he did not want. *How simple our lives would have been but for the interference of our parents,* she mused as she tried to rub some feeling into her stubborn feet. She sat there staring into vacancy, thinking of nothing, aware only of the approaching dawn. Not much could be seen through the small paneless window on one of the walls, but soon the human noises of early risers reached her. No doubt some of the women were setting out for the stream.

Okoboshi turned in his straw bed, looked at her blankly then, recollecting the events of the night, let out a guffaw.

"This is going to be an extremely busy day for you, my educated bride. Get out and find a gourd to take to the stream. The older women will ask you what happened and you will have to tell them your story yourself. My father and I and my people will go to your parents with an almost empty keg of palm wine, and we shall present your mother with the clean towel, since there is nothing inside you but shame. I am sorry it has to be me and my family that are landed with doing this. How I wish we had left you alone. After all these months — me working so hard to save for the gunpowder and my mother using all her profits to buy me a bed for my bride. The gods will never smile on you. Out with you!"

He made as if to push her roughly again, but Aku-nna had had enough. She ran to the outer room, almost into the arms of Okoboshi's mother who stood there in the dim early morning, her arms folded across her chest, her face unsmiling. She spat at her and pointed without words at the water gourds. It was then that Aku-nna cried. Bending down to pick up a gourd, she felt the eyes of other women on her back. Okoboshi's sister, who had materialised from somewhere, said:

"Mother, have you not got some old lappa that befits a slave's mistress? I need this one." So saying, she snatched at the new one Aku-nna had been given the previous night and they handed her an old faded one that smelt as if it had been used for tapping oil from kernels. "To think that madman Okonkwo was asking for fully twenty-five pounds for her! I don't know what the world is coming to," the sister-in-law finished in disgust.

"He will be lucky if we pay him ten pounds in ten years. She is an empty shell. The yolk in her has been used to feed vultures. Go on with you, girl! The message of your adventures shall reach your people before you arrive back from the stream."

With this she was pushed outside. There were girls eager to see her, some to pity, most of them to mock and repeat the accusing description of her as an empty shell.

"Why did you do it?" one or two daring girls asked.

"It will kill your mother," another said.

She heard them all, but somehow Aku-nna's mind was too muddled to know what to make of it. She followed them to the stream, lagging behind all the way, overhearing their jeering remarks. She was being pulled along, mechanically, like a being without a will. It was only at the stream that he realised the extent of the beating she had received from her new people. Her mouth burned with pain as she rinsed it out with cold water. She knew that both her eyes must be swollen for she found it difficult to lift her eyelids upwards. Her head was still reeling like that of someone half drunk. She allowed herself to shed a few tears into the silent stream.

Her new in-laws took ages to wash themselves and fetch their water, and she knew that the delay was deliberate. They wanted as many people as possible to take notice of her, to show her up to other younger girls who might be contemplating similar adventures. She thought she saw her friend Obiajulu, but she looked so remote and strange to Aku-nna that it would have been madness to call out to her. Later on, she was convinced it was Obiajulu, for she recognised that lappa with the design of feathers on it that was one of Obiajulu's favourites, but Obiajulu pretended not to see her but hurriedly climbed the hill and disappeared on the path homewards. So this was the degree to which she had disgraced even her friends.

Would Chike reject her too in this her shameful hour? Okoboshi had not bothered to cut off a lock of her hair because it was not worth cutting; she could run away if she wanted, but to where? Her uncle would surely kill her on sight and she could not count on her mother who would not be permitted to make any decision. But if she was forced to live with these people for long, she would soon die, for that was the intention behind all the taboos and customs. Anyone who contravened them was better dead. If you tried to hang on to life, you would gradually be helped towards death by psychological pressures. And when you were dead, people would ask: Did we not say so? Nobody goes against the laws of the land and survives.

She climbed the hills with the women, and they passed many people on their way to the farm or to the stream. Aku-nna was becoming hungry and tired, and her belly longed for food. When

141

they reached home, Okoboshi's mother summoned her into her hut and put her into an inner room. She was abandoned, for the news had been circulated throughout Ibuza. The word was out that she was not a virgin, but only close relatives knew that it was Chike who was supposed to have slept with her. Eventually she grew tired of waiting and fell asleep. Much later, she heard Okoboshi arguing with his mother about her. He wanted Aku-nna to go to the farm and fetch firewood, and his mother told him to show some mercy for the poor girl had suffered enough.

"Then you can keep her as your maid," he said as he stamped out, "because I don't want her as my wife."

"Yes, I shall keep her," his mother called after him.

After some time, Aku-nna was given some roasted yam and salted palm oil. The yam looked appetising though it tasted like chewing-stick, and try as she might, she could not prevent her jaw aching as she ate. She gave up the attempt and simply thanked her mother-in-law.

"You have not eaten anything," Okoboshi's mother said aghast. "You will faint from hunger, do you know that?"

"Thank you," Aku-nna murmured, looking away quickly, suspicious of this sudden change of heart in a woman who only a few hours before had spat on her.

Okoboshi's mother looked at her with pity. "You know something?" she asked, with a ghost of the smile she had beamed at the new bride the night before. "Do you know what the mother bug told her young?"

Aku-nna shook her head.

"Then I will tell you. The mother bug told her young that hot water doesn't remain hot for long; it turns cold after a while. So take heart. This will blow over. I have known happily married women who started out just like you, on the wrong foot." She picked up the earthenware bowl containing the palm oil and yam, and moved away towards the door.

Aku-nna heard her welcoming somebody outside, calling the person her "little in-law", and, craning her neck to look, saw with surprise that it was her young brother Nna-nndo. He entered, looking sad, and she could tell that he had been crying. The sight of him set her off again, and she wept quietly. Nna-nndo watched her with swollen eyes, looking like a child who had not eaten for days, then he tried to console her.

"Don't cry, sister. I know everything they have said about you isn't true. I wish our father had not died. We would still be in Lagos. I hate that man Okonkwo for marrying our mother. I hate this town, I hate what they are doing to you. But please don't cry, all is not lost. Chike asked me to give you this. All is not lost. He cares for you, he still cares for us."

"Shh. . . . Don't talk so boldly — they may be listening." She snatched the letter from him and read it eagerly. Chike's message was short: he still loved her; she should listen for his whistle after dark when she went to the *owele* in the bush. She should tear up the letter immediately and give the pieces to Nna-nndo, or put them on a fire, if there was one nearby. There was no fire around so she gave her brother the torn pieces, and just in time, too, for the next second Okoboshi marched in in all his arrogance. He swept a disdainful look over Aku-nna and condescended to enquire of Nna-nndo if all was well at home. He went on to remark on his loyalty to his sister, after the shameful way she had treated them all.

In Ibuza, everybody knew that on the day of blood relations, friends would go, and something inside Nna-nndo, though he was little over thirteen, told him that Aku-nna was the closest living relative he had.

He retorted angrily:

"My sister has not shamed anyone. They're all lies, the rumours you have been spreading all day to bring dishonour to our name. Just watch out. If you don't control your tongue, all your sisters will be treated the same way. You girl stealer! You cripple! You, who have not the courage to court and compete for the girl you want, but have to crawl and kidnap her like a rat steals food!"

"I don't want your slut of a sister. When I marry the girl of my choice I shall court her, and she will not be an empty thing who has been messing around with slaves. And I am not lying, she said so herself. Did you not?" he demanded menacingly as he approached Aku-nna.

"If you dare to touch her I shall kill you!" shouted Nna-nndo, grabbing a heavy hand-carved stool belonging to Okoboshi's mother. The latter heard the shouts and dashed in. She took the stool away from Nna-nndo and told her son to leave. Tears of frustration ran down Nna-nndo's cheeks as he strode out of the hut to his own home.

143

It was another moonless, dark night, and Okoboshi's mother informed Aku-nna that she must spend it in her son's hut. Aku-nna protested, begging to be allowed to stay just one night in her hut, but the older woman would not hear of it.

"You must keep going to him, until he gets used to you. Who knows, he may even forgive you in the future."

Aku-nna stifled the urge to tell her the truth, to reveal to her that there was nothing for Okoboshi to forgive. The only sin she had committed was that she loved and cared for another. But she suppressed the temptation, remembering that Chike had promised in his note to whistle again for her. If only she could talk to him, just for a brief minute. . . . Her mother-in-law began to urge her to be on her way, and as the urges threatened to turn into shouts Aku-nna quickly said that she had to go first to the *owele* to ease and tidy herself.

"Yes, go, and don't come back here. Go to your husband's hut!"

Aku-nna walked unhappily to the *owele*, thankful that at least she was allowed to go alone, unlike the night before when she had been chaperoned by her sister-in-law. For Okoboshi had not admitted to his people that he did not actually sleep with her, or they would have asked him, "How then could you know that she was not a virgin?" If he had said he had gone by what Aku-nna herself told him, his father would have seen through it all. But pride would not let Okoboshi speak the whole truth; the snarl and jeer in Aku-nna's confession had cut deep. But this night he was determined to find out for himself. He had told his mother to send the girl to him, that he had changed his mind; he would manage with her until he was able to save and pay the bride price for the wife of his choice.

Aku-nna realised that she had been fortunate that first night. She was worried, however, on behalf of Chike. His people would certainly have heard that she was not a virgin, but Ibuza rumours were always very selective and it would not have been mentioned that she had named their son as her lover. She was so anxious about it that again she could not eat the pounded yam which had been given to her as an evening meal. If death was going to be the easiest way out, she did not mind dying now. Her heart was heavy with foreboding when she heard the whistle again.

The whistling went on, and she stood still listening to it and looking about her. A few stars were peeping shyly from behind the thick dark clouds. There was a movement by the bush very near the *owele*, and before she knew what was happening she was being held tightly by Chike. For a moment he seemed to breathe life into her, giving her exhausted body the energy it lacked, then as suddenly as he had embraced her, he moved away, and all she could hear was his low voice, urgent and insistent.

"Come on, my own — run!"

She did not ask where he was taking her, how long it would take. His command was for her to run, and this she did until tiredness overtook her, and they had to walk. He made her put on a pair of sandals from the hold-all he was carrying on his back like Christian in *Pilgrim's Progress*. He did not stop with the sandals — Aku-nna wondered why the shoes had occurred to him before the dress; maybe his confused mind warned him that snakes lurked in the shadows on moonless nights. He brought out the dress when they were a few miles from Ibuza, and helped her into it. She told him she could not go on any more; but he had thought of everything, even food, though she was not hungry, too weary to eat.

The distance between Ibuza and Asaba was only seven miles but it took nearly four hours to walk it. When they arrived at the house of the driver who was to take them to Ughelli in the morning, Aku-nna at last took refuge in passing out completely. When she came round, she was still in the flowered dress and still in Chike's arms.

10

Tempting Providence

Ben Adegor had been a contemporary of Chike's at St Thomas's Teacher Training College in Ibuza in the late forties. During the four years since they had parted at the end of the course, and Adegor returned to teach in Ughelli, the town in the mid-west region of Nigeria where he was born, they had corresponded constantly and Chike in his letters had written of his feelings for Aku-nna and of his doubts about furthering his education. Adegor suggested that Chike apply to join the big oil company in Ughelli, for he had passed the necessary "A" level subjects; he pointed out that Ughelli and the neighbouring towns of Warri and Sapele held much promise for a young man as a result of recent good prospects for the discovery of oil on their outskirts.

Chike had toyed many a time with going there but was unable to bring himself once and for all to make up his mind until he was quite certain that he would be sharing his life with Aku-nna and nobody else. He had written in advance to the oil company to elicit the promise of an interview; that had been weeks ago, and still he had not heard anything definite from them. One thing, at least, he knew he could count on was Adegor's undertaking to secure a position for Aku-nna in the school where he worked. He had also told Chike he could offer them temporary accommodation in his old hut, now that he had bought a new zinc-roofed house from an Ibo trader who having made his pile of money among the Urhobos was returning to the Eastern Region to start another business in transport. This was a type of venture into which many Nigerians seemed to be rushing as the country moved towards self-government in the fifties, and this Ibo trader, Mr Chima by name, had succeeded in buying out a foreign firm which was leaving prompted by rumours of approaching Independence. Mr Chima sold his house at Ughelli to Adegor, who because of his marriage to his little wife Rose had chosen to abandon the hut he had originally built as a home for himself. This was the hut, which in fact was larger than many houses in the area, that he would put at the disposal of his friend Chike. It was these hopes and expectations, joined with the fact that like the philosopher Kant he believed in the basic rationality and goodness of his fellow man, that persuaded Chike to choose Ughelli as the town in which he would make Aku-nna his bride.

Ben Adegor was a small man, very dark and thickset. He was by nature argumentative, though liking to smile a great deal, and you could never win a point against him for he was the type who never gave in. His tribe, the Urhobos, were reputed to be trouble-makers, yet for as long as Chike had known him Adegor had been a man of his word. His young wife was not too tall, either, although her small-boned frame seemed to give her more height than her sturdy husband. She was a junior teacher in the Ughelli Church Missionary Society school of which he was the headmaster.

Chike had sent word, through a trader friend of his father's, to Ben Adegor that luck had deserted him and that he would be coming after all. He had sent the message in despair on the very night Aku-nna was kidnapped. He told himself that, whatever happened, he was leaving Ibuza for good, and the thought that he could be forced to leave the town without Aku-nna never occurred to him — it was an unthinkable thought. As far as he was concerned, he was leaving, and he was taking Aku-nna with him, even if she had been married to twenty Okoboshis.

Adegor and Rose, who was not much older than Aku-nna and was pregnant, were expecting them, and their joy at seeing the new arrivals only a day after receiving the message was so transparent that Chike stopped feeling guilty at their empty start. He hinted this to his friend, but Adegor had patted him on the back, assuring him that he had got himself all the wealth he needed — Aku-nna. Adegor's stay in Ibuza had been long enough for him to know the risk that Chike, with his background, was running in marrying a girl from there. He promised to listen to the details later; meanwhile he and his wife busied themselves to make their guests comfortable. They showed them to the thatched hut, which was bigger than any hut Aku-nna had seen in Ibuza; Chike explained to her that his friend had originally planned it as a real house, with the hope of zincing the roof later, but had changed

147

his mind when the opportunity to buy the new one from the trader had arisen.

The hut was bare, with three large and airy rooms and a piazza at the back. There was an equally airy veranda at the front. Straight away, Aku-nna fell for this thatched hut — all this openness, just for the two of them! It was a big step forward from the one-room apartment in which she had been brought up as a child in Lagos, and compared to the cave-like hut she and her family shared in Ibuza it was a palace. She felt like throwing her arms wide and singing from room to room, but she restrained herself and allowed her joy to show on her face.

"I shan't have to clay this floor — it's cemented," she remarked happily. The others laughed and agreed with her that claying mud floors every morning was a killing job.

After lending them some pieces of basic furniture, the Adegors left. Chike and Aku-nna were deliriously happy. He couldn't stop kissing her, asking her if she regretted their move, because she could always go back. As she came to realise that Chike was still not all that sure of her feelings toward him, Aku-nna suppressed her own shyness and flung her arms round his neck. She quoted wrongly that portion of the Old Testament of the Bible which said: "Wherever thou goest, I will go. Your people shall be my people and your God my God." That pleased him and he sighed with contentment, brushing his lips against her forehead.

To Rose's disappointment they did not eat much, but they asked her to show them where the Ughelli market and shops were.

"There is a small market here, but if you want to buy hardware you have to go to Warri. There is a regular bus that goes to Warri or Sapele from here."

When Rose left, they started to count their treasures like small children. Mr Ofulue, Chike's father, had encouraged his son in the elopement and had given him a lump sum of one hundred pounds to start life with. Chike also had a small savings account which was still in the Ibuza post office.

"It can be transferred to this place when we are settled in," he said.

"But all that money," Aku-nna gasped. "I've never seen so many currency notes."

"Don't forget that he wanted to pay my way through university."

"And you changed your plans?"

"Universities don't run away. It can wait for me until I'm ready. Right now, I am too busy to think of University." He laughed happily. "Guess what Father said when he gave me this money? You just guess."

"That you shouldn't lose it? Did he tell you to spend it wisely? Oh, yes, I know — he said you should pay my bride price with it." The seriousness with which Aku-nna said the latter startled him.

She lowered her eyes and her lips trembled.

He put the pile of notes down on the table and took her in his arms, telling her not to worry, his father would pay the bride price in good time. His family would pay double whatever Okonkwo asked. He reminded her, however, that the most important people who should benefit from her marriage were her brother and her mother.

"Nna-nndo must come to live with us. That way we shall make sure he gets the proper education he should be receiving. And we must find a way of sending small sums to your mother, so that she can be independent of that man."

"Oh, will you do all that for me? I shall serve you till I die. I shall be a good wife to you. I shall always love you and love you, in this world and the next and the next one after that until the end of time."

He laughed into her hair. "To hear you say that people might think you are marrying me for my money."

"Oh, no, not because of that, but for many other things — your kindness, your understanding and respect for people, and the fact that you are suffering too, I mean your whole family. Oh, I don't know — I want to marry you for many, many reasons which I feel in my heart, although I can't name them all. Your money may make our life, and the life of my people, comfortable but it will be only an added comfort, not the main happiness."

They had had very little sleep, for the driver had left Asaba early and they had arrived in Ughelli by nine in the morning, but the excitement of escaping made them forget their weariness. Chike decided that he would have to go to Warri to get some of the things they would need, and Aku-nna said she would like to go with him, though she was beginning to realise how tired she was.

"My father gave us this money to buy something very special. And that's just what I am going to buy, and we shall christen it tonight."

"What is it, then? Tell me, since I can't guess what it is."

"If I tell you now, you will think I come from a corrupt family. So you just have to wait. You go and stay with Rose, while I go to Warri. I shall stop by the Esso office at the same time, to let them know I am now here in Ughelli and will be available for an interview."

"But don't people put on their best clothes for interviews?"

"They do. I am only going to tell them that I'm here. I have some clean shirts in that hold-all. I'll have to make do with those until my suitcases are brought tomorrow."

Aku-nna did not like the idea of being left behind, with no one but Adegor's wife.

"But you will be dead from fatigue if you come with me," Chike had protested, but she insisted that she was going with him and he had to give in.

The great gift which Mr Ofulue had given them the money to buy happened to be a bed. It was a lovely Vono bed, with a real sprung mattress. Aku-nna did not know what to make of it all, their choosing the sheets, the curtains, the cooking pots and plates and the small oil stove. All these were unfamiliar to her. Even in her father's house in Lagos she never slept in a bed except when she was ill, and that bed had a mattress made of straw and covered with jute bags. If she had agreed to be Okoboshi's wife last night she would have slept on this same kind of bed, though Okoboshi's had been made in Ibuza and was very narrow compared to this one. She was so embarrassed that she wished she had not come with Chike after all, but he was full of confidence, asking her to sit on this mattress or try out that, asking her whether she liked the one with the iron headboard or the wooden one. Finally they chose the iron one because, as Chike wisely pointed out, they did not know how long they would be staying in Adegor's hut and in such places polished wood might attract bugs. He also bought her two whole pieces of lappa material, one with the pattern of fishes on it and the other one known locally as "Abada Record" because of the design of gramophone records drawn on it; it was the latest fashion. She kept thanking him, over and over again, until he made her promise

150

never to say one more thank-you. He touched her cheek when he said this, and saw that she winced involuntarily.

"Were you beaten there last night, on your cheek, I mean?" he asked, looking away at the people in the Warri market square. "That was one of the reasons I did not want you to come with me here, because your face is still slightly swollen."

Aku-nna touched the place on her cheek; yes, it still hurt her but she had tried to ignore it, happy to be free. She begged him to buy her a mirror and he did so, making her promise not to use it until the next day. As they sat in the lorry that was taking them home to Ughelli, he again asked whether she had been badly hurt in the night. She shivered, and he noticed it, but she dodged the question and told him not to talk about it until after he had seen his future employers. The driver agreed to wait for ten minutes while Chike went to the office.

The driver began to fume at Aku-nna when Chike had stayed away exactly thirty minutes, but she pleaded with him to be patient with them. They were just about to get married, she explained — did he not see all the luxurious things they were taking home with them? After all, the driver would have waited two hours if need be, for he knew it was not every day he would have the chance to give a helping hand to people with so much money and so bright a future. It was a proud Chike who at last came out of the oil company's office. He rushed up and made an exuberant grab at her, which made her ache a little; yes, her body was tired. She asked what had happened and he told them all that he was due to start work on the following Tuesday, "exactly five days from today." Aku-nna could not believe their luck, and at the same time fear began to descend on her. Things were working too well and too quickly for them, and she prayed inwardly to God to help them preserve their joy. The driver was given two bottles of Star lager beer from the carton they had bought, and this made him forget about the delay. All of a sudden he became a prophet, and told them that he foresaw nothing but happiness for the two of them.

"Who said marriage is not a bed of roses?" he cried. "As you sow in marriage, so you reap!" If a couple planted rose seeds marriage could be a bed of roses, and it could be a bed of thorns if they planted thorns. He could see that they were sowing roses, for had they not bought the best bed in town? He said he would baptise the bed for them, and accordingly, when they unloaded the bed in front of their new home, he poured half a bottle of beer on it.

"Of course, this is not a proper baptism," he said. "You will do the proper one at night, when you are alone."

Adegor, who was just coming home from his farm, joined in the spirit of the game. People did not baptise without giving names, Adegor said and asked the couple what they were going to call their bed. Aku-nna almost collapsed with laughter and Chike said he had never heard of a bed being given a name before. So Adegor sent for some kolanuts and prayed there on the veranda of the thatched house that the Lord might bless the bed with many children and that those who slept on it would find complete contentment in each other.

"Therefore I christen this bed 'Joy'!"

Everyone laughed and applauded, and Aku-nna got to meet many of their neighbours. For a long time none of them knew her real name but she was nicknamed "the lady who sleeps in the golden bed".

Love-making, to Chike's surprise, did not come naturally to either of them. Aku-nna began by trying to avoid it. First of all she wanted a bath, then she was going to listen to the bush radio they had bought, then she was going to do this and then that. As for Chike, when he had been playing the part of rescuing her from Okoboshi it had all seemed so easy. He would make her his wife, no matter what they had done to her. It was very clear then. He had to admit that his faith in her had wavered when the news came that she was not a virgin, but he still knew that he must have her, even if she was expecting Okoboshi's child. His father had been perceptive enough to warn him of this possibility; he was told never to rebuke a woman for something that had happened in the past, that it was the future that mattered. And Chike had told his father that all he wanted was the girl's heart and happiness, and as long as he had those there was little else he desired.

That had been only last night. But tonight he was faced with making love with either the innocent girl he had known months ago or a woman who had been so badly used that she could not bear to talk about it. He would have felt better if they had been able to talk about it, but she did not want to. When the music on the radio died down, he pulled her up from one of the chairs the Adegors had lent them.

"Remember what that driver said? Well, we mustn't disappoint him." He felt his old confidence returning.

"I know," Aku-nna answered, her mouth shaking and her teeth chattering as if she had a bad cold. "I'm just frightened, that's all."

He almost felt like saying, "You may not be very experienced, my girl, but surely we both know I am not the first," but he remembered his father's advice. Instead he said aloud:

"Come on, my wealth, I'll warm you up and you won't be frightened any more." He wanted to get this first experience with her over fast, so that he could concentrate on just loving her, for what she was, the only girl in his life. What did it matter if he was not her first man? He marvelled that she was still only sixteen. Yes, he had himself had his adventures in Ibuza, but they had usually been with grown-up women with husbands of their own.

She was now trembling so violently that he was becoming disturbed himself. Something in her helpless state stirred the kindness in him.

"I shan't hurt you," he said thickly. "Just relax. How is a man supposed to hurt the very air he breathes, the very joy of his life, his very being . . ."

On and on he went, murmuring sweet nothings to her, until suddenly he realised that his difficulty in entering her was real. He made several attempts and at one of them she cried out in so much pain that he stopped.

"But why?" he had to ask. "You are not a virgin . . ."

A feeling something like cool water spread over her. "But I am," she replied with pride. She might come from a poor family, but she would never bring dishonour to the man she loved. "I have been waiting for you to teach me."

Chike sat up and stared at her. "But Okoboshi said . . ."

"I am sorry, I had to tell him that to get away from him. I even said it was you who did it. Did they not tell you that?"

"And you suffered all that disgrace for nothing, knowing you were innocent?"

"I love you, Chike. Please teach me how to give you joy."

"Your people must know of this," he said. "Your name must be cleared. My father must be told. This is scandalous!"

"Is that all necessary? Since you know now, is it so important that they know as well? Just give them their bride price in peace, because you know what they say: if the bride price is not paid, the bride will die at childbirth."

He shuddered at this and felt like weeping, remembering the picture of her standing at the stream like a young widow in an old lappa.

"Teach me," he heard her now saying drowsily.

It was harder and more painful to her than he expected, but in the morning they both felt better for it. She was still shy of him, of her own outspokenness, but he on the other hand tried to encourage her to speak her wants to him. Soon she learned how he wanted her to give him pleasure.

In Ibuza there was little joy for all associated with Aku-nna. As soon as Okoboshi realised that she had escaped, and with his old enemy, he told his parents not only that he had slept with the girl the night before and found her empty but that he had cut a lock of her hair — some stray curls were produced as evidence — and so, according to their laws and customs, she could not get away from her husband. This created long arguments, and many of Aku-nna's people got really angry with the Ofulues. They openly asked them if they had forgotten who they were and accused them of ruining the life of a young and innocent girl. She could never now return to Ibuza because she had committed an abomination. Some elders, however, pointed out that as long as Okonkwo did not accept any bride price from the slave, the girl still belonged to Okoboshi for no one in his senses would use the same standards to judge the deeds of a slave and those of the son of a free man. This disappointed Okoboshi, for he intended that Aku-nna would never again reach Ibuza with her slave lover. There were threats against Chike's sisters and his parents. His father did not fear for his own life but he sent all the girls of the family away until things quietened down. They took their revenge on him in another way.

Years before, when Mr Ofulue had retired as a headmaster, he had returned to Ibuza, the town of his birth. He accepted that he

154

was of slave ancestry and would antagonise the people on that score; but he did not mind. Ibuza was the only town in which he had roots. He planted cocoa beans and palm trees and coconut palms on the piece of land that he bought, and this caused a great deal of jealousy as the people could see that he began to reap the fruits of his labours. This plantation was a sensitive spot with Ofulue, and it was exactly here that he was hit. He simply woke up one morning to find all his plants hewed to the ground. The shock of it did not kill the old man off but it shook him badly. Left to him, he would have let sleeping dogs lie, since it would be impossible to discover who the culprit was, but his sons did not agree. They might not be able to pinpoint who was responsible but they had an idea of who had originated the plot. So Ofulue's sons and daughters pooled their resources and sued the Obidi family.

The whole of Ibuza came forward as witnesses against the Ofulues. But the law was based in English justice which did not make allowance for slaves, so the Ibuza people lost the case and were ordered to compensate the Ofulue family in kind. The free men had to plant new cocoa for the slave and the heavy fines were duly paid. This in no way improved the relationship between the people of the town and the Ofulue family. And curses were equally heaped on the family that had started it all, Okonkwo's family.

This was having a bad effect on Okonkwo. Aku-nna, his brother's daughter, had degraded not only her own family but the whole town as well. He became very ill. The oracles knew the cause of his illness. They asked him, "Why did you allow a girl in your care to commit such abominable deeds?" Okonkwo forgot his ambition for the Eze title, and fought for his life and the life of his immediate family. He retaliated on Ma Blackie. In Ibuza, if a man divorced or no longer wanted his wife, he would expose his backside to her in public; and Okonkwo did just that, one evening when the fever was burning in him so fiercely that he scarcely knew what he was doing. He walked like a man without eyes straight into Ma Blackie's hut and shouted, calling all his ancestors to be his witness. He removed his loin cloth and pointed his bare posterior towards Ma Blackie's face. His relatives and friends who stood by covered their faces in shame, for this was not a step commonly taken by Ibuza men. Okonkwo's worried mind must be driving him to the wall.

It was known in Ibuza that if you wished to get rid of someone who lived far away, you made a small doll in the exact image of the person and pierced the heart of the doll with a needle, or alternatively set it alight and allowed it to burn gradually. It was evident that it worked, though nobody was sure how because those who knew the art would not submit it to scientific investigation; the victim usually died, very slowly and very painfully. So it came as no surprise to Ma Blackie to see the image of her daughter one morning in front of Okonkwo's *chi*, his personal god, when she just happened to be passing by. She cried quietly for her daughter, and had to concede to Chike's secret request that Nna-nndo should go to Ughelli. The boy was very willing to go to his sister, especially now that the Ofulues had taken it upon themselves to give his mother a couple of pounds each month. This had made her more independent and she was beginning to live much more comfortably than her former mates and friends. But despite this, she worried about her daughter and knew that unless something desperate was done to prevent it Okonkwo was determined to kill the girl. Ma Blackie knew exactly what she was going to do. She would either bribe Okonkwo into removing the image from the *chi*, or threaten him directly by showing him an image of himself with needles in it. She had enough money now to pay the witch doctors to do that much for her and if they realised that she had the backing of the rich Ofulue family she would be able to rely on their support to help her win. Meanwhile, she could only pray to the God of the Christians to lead her through a safe delivery of her baby and to make the people of Ibuza get over what had happened quickly. She need not have worried on the latter count, for when they saw how well off she looked all her friends came back to her. They were suspicious of where she was getting her money from, but after the recent court case and the heavy fines they had to pay, no one was saying anything.

In Ughelli, Aku-nna and her husband were enjoying what seemed to be an endless honeymoon. Nna-nndo was established in school there and was growing fast, now that he had regular food and richer surroundings. After their marriage at the local registry office, Chike and his bride had moved to a more sophisticated house, taking their bed "Joy" with them. They still lived within walking distance of Ben Adegor and his wife, and the drunken lorry driver had become a useful friend and helper. Aku-nna would not hear of giving up her teaching career now that Chike was being trained to be a manager in the oil firm.

"I know they only pay me five pounds a month, but that buys our food and it gives me something to do when the house is quiet," she rationalised.

Chike had to acquiesce, but somehow he was worried about her. She was a loving wife, very content in many ways, yet it seemed sometimes that a shade of unhappiness passed through her mind. She was very transparent in her moods, one of those people whose thoughts were easy to read; yet whenever Chike asked her if anything was the matter, she would rush to him, leaving whatever she was doing, and swing her arms about his neck, and ask him in turn whether he was happy with her. She had this peculiar way of dodging the issue, and Chike concluded that maybe these bouts of melancholy were just part of her.

"You cannot expect a person to be happy all the time of the day, just because they happen to be married to you."

So he let her be. He suspected that she might be worried that her bride price was not being paid. Chike's father knew that Okonkwo was planning evil for his new daughter-in-law but he kept this knowledge from the young people. When Ma Blackie had informed him about Aku-nna's image on the *chi* in front of Okonkwo's house, he had made her promise not to let her daughter know.

"Most of these things do little harm if the intended victim is not aware of them," he had said with worldly experience.

Still, Chike's persistence had moved him to offer Okonkwo a bride price of fifty pounds, double the amount that Ibuza custom originally stipulated, before the sum had been inflated by greedy fathers. Okonkwo had refused and, to add insult, made Ofulue understand that he had not given his daughter to any slave. Ofulue thought that he would offer the money again in the future, when tempers had cooled. He would offer a hundred pounds then and, as he confided to his son in a letter, he was sure Okonkwo would accept. He was an incurable optimist, Mr Ofulue.

Chike broke this discouraging news to Aku-nna as gently as he could. He left out the unpalatable details and quickly destroyed

157

the letter. She cried a little, and murmured,

"I wonder why people hate one another so? Do you think my own father would have been so bitter?"

"No, my love, your father could not have been so bitter. Your brother Nna-nndo must take after him; he has an awful temper but does not bottle up wrongs for long. Your uncle is different. He is a frustrated man."

She smiled through her depression at the recollection of her father, with his tiny voice, and remembered the day he had thrown a glass at her Uncle Uche, almost slicing his ear. Yet when he knew he might be dying, it was to this very prodigal nephew that he told the truth, not his children, because he knew they were too young. She placed her head on her husband's shoulder and he loved her into sleep.

But her quiet spells still persisted. Then he came from work one afternoon to be met at the door by Nna-nndo instead of Aku-nna, who usually rushed to him, and he immediately asked where she was.

"She came back early from school because her head ached," Nna-nndo explained. "She is asleep."

Yes, she was sleeping. Seeing her lying there so small and helpless, like a child, Chike noticed that she had not gained any weight at all. He wondered. Nna-nndo had almost doubled his size since coming to live with them, but Aku-nna was getting nowhere. In fact he had noted during the past weeks that she was tiring more and more easily. When they made love, she accepted him with gentle pleasure but it was up to him to do all the asking and the giving. It had not been so at the beginning. Most of the time she had pestered him, until he laughed and told her he would not give in unless she had been extra good during the day. It had been like a little game they both played, and he had enjoyed it. Now she always waited for him to ask and would fall asleep immediately afterwards; on some mornings she was even too tired to get up as early as she usually did. He went to the edge of the bed now and sat down beside her. He touched her head, and it was so hot that he drew his breath in with a soft whistle of alarm.

She opened her eyes and said, "Welcome home. I'm sorry I overslept and was not at the door to welcome you back. Have you eaten? I asked Nna-nndo to get your food ready for you. I don't feel too well."

He kissed her hot brow. "What is it? That other pain?" He tried to inject some lightheartedness into a situation which was beginning to worry him.

"No," she replied, smiling with difficulty. "Come to think of it, I haven't had that pain for a long time now. Not since Christmas. And that pain was always in my back and lower tum, not the head."

"You must forgive me — I never learn," he apologised cheerfully. Then he held her wrist and frowned. "You say the last time was at Christmas?"

"I think so. Yes, you remember, after the party at your office, when we both were drunk. You remember."

Yes, he remembered all right, because she had ruined a dress they had both looked forward to her wearing. Luckily he noticed it before others did, and had to pretend they were drunk as an excuse to rush her home in time. He remembered.

"Look, Akum, that was three months ago. Aren't you supposed to have it every month?" He studied her closely then blurted out, "You can't be pregnant, can you?"

"I don't see why not," she giggled, covering her face with the bedclothes. "Mrs Adegor told me so this afternoon when she saw me home. I hope she is right, because I shall be very happy to have a child of my own. Will you not be happy too?"

"Of course, I shall be very happy. I am already very happy, so it will be an added bonus." He sat her up, with her feverish head resting on his shoulder, and, like any young parents-to-be, they planned what they were going to call their son. As far as Chike was concerned it must be a boy, and she hoped it would be, but tentatively asked if he would be disappointed if it were a girl.

"I won't mind a girl. The only thing is that people would think I make love to you night and day, because girls are love babies. I want our love to be private."

Aku-nna laughed then. "In that case, I shall pray for a girl, and another one after this, and another one. I shall have a boy when you are forty."

"You are a witch."

He led her on to a more serious matter, asking her the question he had meant to ask before. He wanted to know whether it was just the baby that was making her so tired or in fact the whole life they were leading. It was after all quite a busy life, with her teaching all week and endless parties at the weekends with his colleagues at work. She admitted that she had been feeling more tired than usual and thought that perhaps the baby was responsible. She had not thought that pregnancy might be behind it all until that afternoon, when her head had ached so much that she felt dizzy. Her friends at the school had poured cool water on her head, and Adegor the headmaster had sent her home in company of his wife.

"But why didn't you send for me?" Chike rebuked her.

"I am sorry. Adegor suggested that I did, but when I got into bed I fell straight asleep."

The company doctor soon confirmed the fact that their baby was on the way. He warned them, though, that Aku-nna must either completely change her diet and stop work or run the risk of having a difficult time.

"Mr Ofulue, your wife is so young, and so small. She has been undernourished for a long while, so you should have given her time to recuperate after you married before deciding on a baby. Is she sixteen yet?"

"Yes, just," Chike answered, feeling as guilty as ever. Come to think of it, it had never occurred to him that women got pregnant so easily. She had not even known it herself until a few days previously. "She will be all right?"

"Oh, yes. But you must both be very careful. She has hardly enough blood for herself, let alone for a baby, but we shall do our best. I am glad you consulted the clinic early. That may be the saving grace."

When Chike drove her home from the Warri Clinic in the Volkswagen they had just bought, she noticed that he seemed to be annoyed with her, with the car, with the road, with everything. That was the last thing she needed after the endless probes and questions at the clinic, but she did not feel up to asking him what it was that ailed him. The air was cool that evening and on the way back she fell asleep.

She wanted to keep her job. That was the cause of the first actual quarrel they had.

"I must keep working, to contribute towards the amount you spend on my family." She clung to him, begging him to let her stay on at the school, but he pushed her away into a chair.

160

"You mean you want to continue until your bride price is paid," he snarled sarcastically. "Why didn't you say that? How many hours do you spend thinking about your family, your mother, your uncle? You think about them so much that sometimes I think I don't exist for you. Do you ever wonder what it would be like for me if you became ill, maybe too ill even to care for our child? I shall see that that bride price is paid, if it's the last thing my father ever does for me. And you are not going to die and leave me. Do you understand?"

She was frightened now. Was she going to die? Had the doctor said so?

"Please tell me," she cried out aloud, "please, my husband, tell me. Did the doctor say I am going to die? Was that why you were so upset? Was that . . ."

He went back to her, contrite, and held her in his arms, kissing her head. "No, I'm sorry, I was only voicing my own fears. The doctor didn't say that, but he hinted that if we are not careful things may not work out as we hope they will. I don't want anything to happen to you — can't you see that you are my heart? Please don't let me quarrel with you."

Months later, Aku-nna asked herself what had ever given her the idea that she could have combined her teaching with looking after her brother and her husband. The baby was giving her a very difficult time. Her sickness in the mornings and the loss of appetite went on for months; she still had not regained her appetite even though she was now in her sixth month of pregnancy. It saddened her that she was causing her young husband so much anxiety. His eyes looked worried and pained every time he made love to her, which he did as gently as if she were an egg that might crack at any touch. He had even arranged for a local girl to come in to do their cooking. All Aku-nna had to do was simply to see to the smooth running of things, to occupy herself by reading as many light novels as she could find, and to eat foods that would enrich her blood. Chike's brother who was a gynaecologist had visited them on his way to Ibuza and had confirmed what the other doctor had said.

"It is almost as if something or other were sucking away her blood," he confided to his brother in despair.

161

"But what is it? Most girls of her age in Ibuza have babies. Why should it be so painful for the very girl I love? She is getting weaker every day as the baby grows in her."

"Don't worry. If it comes to the crunch, they can always operate and save both the mother and her child. And remember that most girls of her age who have babies in Ibuza do survive, but a quarter of them still die due to lack of medical treatment and as a result of bad feeding in their youth. Your wife could pass for a fourteen-year-old. You should have waited as you were advised — but it's too late to talk about that now. After this child, she should not have any more until she is at least twenty-two."

Chike gave a short and bitter laugh. "The irony is that we did not even plan this one. It just happened. It never occurred to me that she could be pregnant. She is so young, maybe that's why we were careless. She did not even realise herself that she was pregnant until a friend told her."

"I shouldn't worry now. She is in good hands and very happy as well," observed his brother.

"Aku-nna has never stopped being happy. She was a bit tense at times, but she is a contented and easily satisfied wife," Chike bragged.

"You are lucky. She is worth the fight you had to go through for her. She's very beautiful, even more so in pregnancy. I like her, so please take good care of her and see that she does all she is told to do." This was the advice of the senior son of the Ofulue family to his brother.

At home in Ibuza, Okonkwo was again approached with the bride price, but he still refused to consent to give his daughter to a slave. When somebody — no one knew who — took away the doll that looked like Aku-nna from in front of his *chi*, he thundered and raged like an animal and was determined to make another one. The new one he made was at a very expensive cost, for its aim was to call Aku-nna back from Ughelli through the wind.

The old man, Chike's father, came to Ughelli to stay for a while with his son and daughter-in-law, and was thrilled to see them so happy. He knew that Aku-nna was carrying her baby with great difficulty, but they did not let that spoil their joy at seeing each other. She and old Ofulue spent the long afternoons when

Chike was at work talking and laughing, and Ofulue was wise enough to remind her when to stop and lie down, and he would tell her funny stories about Ibuza. In that period it was usually an exceptionally happy young wife who welcomed Chike back from his office.

When the time came for Ofulue to go, Aku-nna found herself clinging to him desperately.

"I hope I shall see you again, Father. You see, I know my uncle does not want ever to accept the bride price. He calls me back in the wind, when I am alone. But I shall never answer. I don't want to die, Father."

Ofulue held her, trying to calm her beating heart. He looked over her head to his son who stood by the car watching them both. Chike could not hear what Aku-nna was saying but when he realised that she was crying, he came over and loosened her grip on his father.

"After the baby is born," he consoled her, "we shall all go home together. Father will be looking forward to that."

Aku-nna lowered her eyes, as if she had betrayed her husband. She made herself wave as the car moved off. She was frightened now of being by herself. Over and over again, she heard this voice calling her, telling her she must come back to her family, to her people. Now that Chike's father had gone, she did not know what she would do in those long, lonely hours when the voice called. She had given up reading, for she could no longer concentrate, as the movements of her child became stronger and more frequent. At first the kickings had given her a kind of sweet sensation, but as the days progressed she was finding them slightly painful and uncomfortable. She could not sleep, however much she tried. They had given her some sleeping tablets to take, but what with her dread of the voice and the kicking of the child, rest still completely eluded her.

Chike responded to her moods and sufferings, though he avoided discussion of them except when she brought up the subject. Every night they prayed together to God to help them through this stressful period. But still her fears persisted, so much so that she had begun to call out in her brief phases of sleep. She would suddenly wake up in the night, covered in perspiration, begging Chike to please hold her because somebody, her uncle, was trying to take her away.

"Please, my husband, don't let him take me! Please don't, please!"

Chike often managed to calm her by telling her that it was just that her nerves were bad, that it was the fault of that little person inside her. He assured her that it would all be over very soon, for there were less than two months to go. Frequently she would fall asleep again in his arms as he stroked her now very big stomach, the skin of which was so stretched that he could imagine the discomfort she must be going through whenever she fought for breath. Everything about her seemed stretched to breaking point. On her thin arms the veins stood out in relief. The bout of peaceful sleep would last only an hour or two and then she would be awakened once more by the baby moving and thrusting furiously within her. She would cry gently until the pain eased and she tried to sleep again.

Such nights had become so common that Chike was not taken by surprise when, after one particularly hysterical scream, she passed out. It took him ages to revive her and when eventually she did open her eyes it was as the baby began to assert its right to get out. The first time such an attack took place it was past eleven o'clock at night, and afterwards she dropped off into an exhausted sleep.

"Don't give in, my little sufferer, please don't give in now," he murmured to her. "We have been through such a lot, so please don't give in."

She clasped his hand and smiled drowsily. As soon as it looked as if she was calmed enough to be left in care of her young brother, Chike slipped out to call the doctor. The latter wasted no time. She must be admitted to hospital immediately.

It all happened as if in a dream. Chike stood aside and watched strange men lifting his wife and taking her into the ambulance, saw them covering her with their horrid red blankets. He sat by her, holding on to her damp hand, feeling her every twitch as she sweated through the pains. At the hospital he learned the truth. The birth must be by a Caesarean operation. He was assured that such births did not carry as much danger as they used to. The baby would be premature, but it would be all right.

He waited on one of the chairs in the hospital lounge. He sat there, not seeing anything around him, and his mind went back to the day he had met a little girl of thirteen or so coming home from Lagos with her family — a little girl who had been so shy she could hardly say a word. An innocent child who had not even lived at all yet. He remembered the day they had bought their furniture, the day they had chosen their bed, and how they had counted every penny until he was paid his first salary. He remembered their escape and his fear that Okoboshi had harmed her. He cried quietly, and tears streamed down his cheeks.

A light hand rested on his shoulder, and the hand was shaking, for its owner was also crying. It was Nna-nndo. He had ridden the seven miles to the hospital on his school bicycle, unable to bear being left behind. He sat now beside his brother-in-law who to his young eyes had become the ideal man, his hero, the type of man he hoped he would grow up to be. These past months Nna-nndo had lived with them had inspired him to do better for himself. He had forgotten the crude life of Ibuza, and was thankful to Chike and his sister for making this new existence possible for him. The thought that it might all be coming to an end was too terrible to contemplate. Should anything happen to his beloved sister, everything would change for him. He would be losing a person who had been more like a gentle guardian angle to him and his whole life would be plunged in chaos. With all this going on in his head, Nna-nndo sat silently by his brother-in-law.

Chike looked wordlessly at the profile. Just like his sister's. Funny, that he had not noticed before how alike they were, especially those large eyes, now so troubled in Nna-nndo's head. He looked away, seeing that the boy was crying.

They did not stay thus for long. A doctor, or surgeon — Chike could not at first make out who the man was for his eyes were still misty — stood there by the door of the lounge looking undecided. Then he walked up to them and rather sheepishly introduced himself to Chike as Mr Wood. He was the surgeon in charge of the obstetrics section of the hospital.

"Mr Ofulue?" he enquired with brows arched. "Please come with me."

Chike followed like a sleepwalker. When they were at the door, the surgeon paused and said:

"She has had the operation. She is not yet conscious, and I am afraid the chances are that she may not regain consciousness. I am sorry. We have done everything possible, but she was in an extremely anaemic condition. I don't know how she managed to

165

keep alive till now. I expect you would like to stay with her for a while. We don't know how long she will remain like this." He indicated a door to Chike, and then whispered, "You have a baby girl. She is undersize, but doing fine."

Chike stared blankly at him. Then he walked quickly past him and into the unnaturally clean white room, feeling as though he were entering a shrine. The surgeon left, and he was alone with Aku-nna.

His first reaction was to wonder at the unreality of the situation. Here she was lying still, her eyes closed, her face calm, her body scarcely bigger than that of a child, and all her pains gone. He had not seen her quite like this for a long time now. Now at last she was peaceful, and for a brief second, filled with an illusion of relief, he felt better. At least she was not in pain.

He took the small hand that lay on top of the sheet and held it. Then he brought his lips down near it and kissed it, noticing how dry it had become, how unlike the usual moist living hand of his beloved. Aku-nna was dying and he knew it then. He must call in Nna-nndo; the two of them must stay close by her until the end.

They both sat there, Chike by the edge of the bed, still holding the passive hand, and Nna-nndo on a nearby chair, gazing at the two of them alternately. Dawn was approaching when the hand moved slightly.

A faint but recognisable smile hung on Aku-nna's lips, and then she spoke, very clearly.

"I can feel you here, my husband. I know you are here." Slowly she opened her eyes. They were very bright, those eyes, too bright to be earthly. The brownness of them mingled with some kind of angelic fire that gave them even more beauty.

Nna-nndo, at the sound of her voice, drew nearer, and he too smiled, sadly and hesitantly.

"Don't worry, brother," she said, now rather haltingly. "This isn't the end of the road for you. It is the beginning. Our uncle will not worry you or our mother about the bride price now. My husband will take care of you as long as he possibly can. He is a good man, and God has blessed us with him."

Nna-nndo buried his head by his sister's pillow and began to cry. Aku-nna wanted to cry too, but a funny kind of cough got hold of her. She held her stomach and tried to raise her head up, but she could not. Her hands waved helplessly in the air as she struggled for breath. Chike held her down gently until the spasm was over and she relaxed and collapsed into his arms. He motioned to Nna-nndo with his eyes to move away, and started to wipe his wife's brow, which was suddenly moist.

"My husband and my rock. Be happy, for my sake." Her voice had now grown faint and indistinct, like that of someone talking in sleep. Once more she opened her eyes. "What did we have?"

"A little girl," he replied in her ear.

Then a kind of inner glow, that seemed to defy even death to quench it, spread over her young and tired features. Her sense of humour came back, and she boasted, with so much force, in fact with all the force left in her body:

"I told you so. I told you that I would not keep our love a secret. Now, with our little girl, everybody will know. They will all know how passionately we love each other. Our love will never die. . . . Let us call her Joy too, the same name we gave to the bed on which she was conceived." Her voice assumed a pleading tone. "Please, promise me that you will call her Joy. . . . Promise me that you will be happy, because you have made me so happy, so. . . ."

Her voice had shrunk to a whisper and then disappeared as she seemed to lose consciousness again. Chike gathered her whole body in his arms and kissed her quivering mouth gently.

"Good night, my love. Our child's name shall be Joy."

A smile moved her face again, an almost unearthly smile, and she clutched feverishly at his shirt. The hand started to tremble, and gradually released its grip of him, as she breathed her last. He knew she was gone. But he still held her, tenderly but closely to his heart.

An early cock was crowing somewhere, sounding remote and lonely in the empty morning. Another cock answered from the hospital compound.

The surgeon came into the room. He helped Chike untwine his arms from his wife's body and said. "It's time to go now. She is at peace."

"She shall be called Joy," Chike said as he let go.

167

So it was that Chike and Aku-nna substantiated the traditional superstition they had unknowingly set out to eradicate. Every girl born in Ibuza after Aku-nna's death was told her story, to reinforce the old taboos of the land. If a girl wished to live long and see her children's children, she must accept the husband chosen for her by her people, and the bride price must be paid. If the bride price was not paid, she would never survive the birth of her first child. It was a psychological hold over every young girl that would continue to exist, even in the face of every modernisation, until the present day. Why this is so is, as the saying goes, anybody's guess.